T0128100

THE HARDER
SHE COMES

THE HARDER
SHE COMES
BUTCH/FEMME EROTICA

Edited by
D. L. King

CLEiS
PRESS

Published in the United States by Cleis Press, Inc., 221 River Street, 9th Floor, Hoboken, NJ 07030

Printed in the United States.
Cover design: Scott Idleman/Blink
Cover photograph: Phyllis Christopher
Text design: Frank Wiedemann
First Edition.
10 9 8 7 6 5 4 3 2 1

Trade paper ISBN: 978-1-57344-778-2
E-book ISBN: 978-1-57344-781-2

Contents

INTRODUCTION

Everything is circular. Things go in and out of fashion and everything old becomes new again. I remember commenting on my mother's hopelessly out-of-date wardrobe and she said, "Just wait, it'll come back." And, of course, she was right. She had some totally cool shoes that were, sadly, a half size too big for me.

I don't like being told what I can and can't do.

There was a time, for a while there, when I couldn't identify with being a feminist. These days, however, feminism doesn't necessarily imply that people have to act a certain way, say certain things, or belong to a certain gender to call themselves feminists. It doesn't even imply that they have to wear 100% cotton or be vegan, so I can get behind it again.

It wasn't very long ago that the notion of butch/femme relationships fell out of favor in the eyes of the Powers That Be, or those who fancied themselves as such. Of course really, women, since time immemorial, have been loving women in all sorts of varied and beautiful ways and, thankfully, nothing will ever change that. We are who we are. The politicization of the butch/ femme relationship, as with all things circular, is back in favor again, allowing us to be out and proud and celebrate our butch/ femme selves.

The Harder She Comes does just that, and in many and varied ways. Never let it be said that any book of mine would imply that there was only one true way to celebrate the butch/ femme mystique. Here you will find suave, sexy daddies and adorable little girls who know what they want and how to go about getting it, like in Evan Mora's "Speakeasy." You'll also find bottom bois who dream of getting it on with sexy femme tops and maybe even sexy butch tops in Miel Rose's "Farmhand."

There are butches who pass and femmes who demand perfect obedience from their boys. You'll find a butch tattoo artist who's turned on by the semi-naked girls she inks and what happens one night when the femme in her chair won't take no for an answer in Crystal Barela's "Tits Down, Ass Up." What about wanting something that definitely *isn't* politically correct? Sinclair Sexsmith masterfully explores that idea in "Good Girl, Bad Girl." (Is it getting hot in here?)

The Harder She Comes is about knowing what you want and what you need and not letting anyone, including yourself, stand in your way of getting it. I think CS Clark says it best in "This Is What I Want:"

And this, this is exactly what I want. Both of us like this and every other way we can think of being. Do it again.

D. L. King
New York City

SPEAKEASY

Evan Mora

'm tapping out a steady beat, my heels a metronome on the
quiet city street. I feel conspicuous in my vintage-inspired
fringed silver dress, but a quick scan of the sidewalks tells me
that no one's paying any attention. I keep up my pace, though,
because the colors are bleeding out of the warm September
dusk, and in this less gentrified part of town where hip restaurants rub shoulders with titty bars and rooms by the hour, a girl
still has to take care.

I'm a little breathless—though who can tell if it's from the
brisk walk or the anticipation—when my destination comes
into view: What Are You Looking At?, the standoffishly named,
east-side hipster lounge and sometimes-home of the lusciously
divine Butch/Femme Salon. Tonight's salon theme is the roaring
'20s, and two finely muscled studs flank the doorway like a pair
of gangsters. My heart does a little flip as I'm treated to openly
appreciative once-overs.

"Good evening, ma'am," says the one on the left, her sensual
lips curving into a smile.

"Gentlemen." I incline my head in greeting while the one on the right opens the door, all bedroom eyes and promise.

It *feels* illicit, even though it's not. It feels like secret pass-words and shady alleys, like I'm crossing the threshold into a throwback blending of a Prohibition-era speakeasy and a lesbian bar from the '50s. But even that doesn't begin to describe the deliciousness of a scene where every masculine-of-center flavor imaginable—butches, Daddies, papis, studs, aggressives, trans-folk, and bois—are all dressed to the nines in their suits and ties, their wingtips shined and their fedoras creased just so. It's enough to make a femme heart flutter.

Despite the name, the place itself is quite inviting. The long, narrow front room is a patchwork of exposed brick, painted concrete, and floor-to-ceiling windows—a modern parlor, if you will—with twinkling red chandeliers and black leather chairs and sofas, all filled with girls and their beaus huddled close together, and the sounds of their giggles and low whis-pers. But it's the back room where I'm headed, where the crowd congregates, beckoned by the burnt orange glow of the bar and the smooth sounds of jazz filling the room, turned down just enough to keep conversation possible.

I sidle up to the bar and order a dirty martini and before you can say *everything's Jake*, someone else sidles up next to me, and I'm staring into the bluest blue I've ever seen, and it just gets better from there. Sandy blond hair swept casually across the forehead above aristocratic brows, high cheekbones, full lips, and a chiseled jaw. Oh my.

"Hello, gorgeous."

"Well, hello yourself," I reply.

"Is this seat taken?" There's flirtation in those eyes.

"It's available," I say coyly.

"Good. Because if you were saving it for someone…"

"Honey," I cut to the chase, "it's available, and so am I." I'm treated to a dazzling smile that I can't help but return before adding: "But I don't drink with strangers."

"I'm Jay," she says, with a slight incline of her head.

"As in 'Gatsby'?"

"Only less tortured." She laughs, and it's infectious, and I find myself laughing too.

"Evie." I offer my name in return, and Jay captures my hand and brushes my knuckles with her warm, soft lips.

"It's a pleasure to make your acquaintance, Evie." For a moment, the laughter in her eyes is replaced by something entirely different, and awareness dances across my skin like the faintest of touches, sending shivers racing inward.

There are a lot of gangsters in the room tonight, but not this one; this one's all class, from her pin-striped black suit and double-breasted waistcoat to her perfectly pressed white shirt and perfectly knotted silver tie, right down to the gorgeous silver cufflinks that fasten her French cuffs (did I mention I'm a sucker for French cuffs?). There isn't a femme in her right mind that wouldn't be flattered to have the attentions of so fine a butch specimen, and I lean in a little closer, putting my ample attractions on display, place a hand on her sleeve, and look up through my lashes with a sultry little smile.

A lot can be said without saying a thing; entire conversations can be had. There is a language we speak, without any words, filled with nuance and the subtleties of body language. In that beat of time, the tone of our interaction changes, and when Jay speaks again, her tone is decidedly different.

"So tell me why a beautiful girl like you is out here all alone instead of home with her Daddy where she belongs?"

"I don't have a Daddy." I pout just a little, but it's an act and she knows it.

"Is that so?" She says, tracing a finger across my bare shoulder and down my arm.

"Mmm-hmm." I worry my lower lip between my teeth, enjoying the look of desire that flashes in her sapphire eyes.

"Well then," Jay says, "I think you'd better stick with me tonight."

"Why's that?"

"Pretty little thing like you out here with no one to take care of her? A lot of boys in this place might take advantage of that. Can't have that now, can we?"

"Uh-uh." I shake my head, all wide-eyed innocence looking up into her knowing eyes.

Someone jostles my bar stool, trying to catch the bartender's attention, but Jay's there to steady me, her hand warm and strong at my elbow.

"This joint's filling up fast," Jay says. "Maybe you should come sit on my lap, hmm? That way no one else bumps into you." I nod sagely, and then Jay's hands are at my waist, lifting me from my stool as though I weigh nothing and settling me gently across her lap.

I'm not one to swoon, but I admit, I have to check the dreamy little sigh that wells up in my chest. Jay's thighs are rock solid beneath me, and she smells like cedar and spice and long nights of passion in front of a roaring fire. I want to curl into her and breathe her in, but I settle for feathering a kiss on her jaw and whispering into her ear.

"Thank you...Daddy." There's hesitation in my voice, and Jay captures my chin between her thumb and forefinger, assessing me intently while my heart beats in my throat.

"You want to be my little girl tonight, Evie?" There's no escaping those penetrating eyes; there's nowhere else to look. I nod; yes, that's what I want.

"Say it," she says.

"I want to be your little girl."

She shakes her head slowly. "Say it nicely."

"Please, Daddy, can I be your little girl tonight?" I feel vulnerable and small and just a little bit scared and aroused all at the same time.

The corner of her sensual mouth curves upward, then her hand slides to the back of my neck and she draws me slowly forward, until my mouth is all but touching hers, so close I can feel the warmth of her breath kissing my lips, and my lips part instinctively beneath hers.

"Okay, babydoll," she whispers into my mouth, "you can be my little girl." She's so close I can taste her, and it's all I can think about, the way her lips will feel on mine, the way her tongue will feel stroking against mine. Jay chuckles softly and leans back, and it's all I can do not to moan with dismay.

"Patience, baby girl, we're just going to move this somewhere a little quieter." Her hands are at my waist again, steadying me as she sets me down and steps off her bar stool. She's taller than me, even with the added height my heels provide, and as she takes my hand and leads me back toward the red-lit parlor, I drink in her broad shoulders and lean build, feeling feminine and curvy and tremendously sexy at her side.

There's a single unoccupied black leather armchair tucked deep into the shadows in the corner of the room, and Jay leads us unerringly toward it. Somehow I'm not surprised; although every other space is occupied, she strikes me as the kind of person who is used to having whatever she wants, whenever she wants it, and I thrill at the thought that right now, she wants me.

Jay sinks into the soft leather, looking up at me with an enigmatic smile. I dither a little bit, because I'm not entirely sure how I'm supposed to arrange myself across her lap. No matter what she may think, this isn't something I do every day, let alone in front of an audience.

"Why don't you straddle my lap, babydoll?" she says, and a blush steals into my cheeks, though I know she can't see it in the low crimson light. I cast a glance around the room; there are three or four other couples kissing and petting on the sofas, and no one's paying us the slightest attention.

"Don't you worry about them, baby," she says, "they're not worried about us."

She's right, and I know it, and she looks so goddamned sexy sprawled in that chair in that moment that I don't think it would matter even if every eye in the room *was* on us, I'd still do exactly what she wanted me to do.

My knees sink into the warm leather on either side of her hips and I lower myself delicately onto her, all too aware of the heat emanating from between my thighs and the substantial bulge tucked into her well-tailored pants. This Daddy has come to the party packed and ready to play, and I stifle a moan against her shoulder when her hands settle on my hips and guide me more firmly onto her just as she rocks her hips upward beneath me.

"You see what you do to me, babydoll?" Jay whispers in my ear, her tongue swirling around the sensitive shell and then retreating, sending shivers down my spine. "You made your Daddy all hard."

Jay's hands are on the move, rounding the curve of my ass, squeezing tightly, venturing lower, to where my ass meets the tops of my thighs, and where the hem of my short flapper dress has come to rest. There's an inch of creamy skin exposed above the tops of my garters, and Jay groans as she discovers both the flesh and the stockings.

"You're a dirty little girl, aren't you, Evie?" Jay's mouth is just beneath mine, and I have an almost obsessive need to kiss her, but I wait, like a good girl, while she strokes me with her hands and her words.

"Dressed up all nice and pretty on the outside, but underneath..." Oh fuck, I want to kiss her so badly... "Underneath, you're just a little slut, aren't you?"

My pussy feels heavy and swollen, engorged with blood and slick with the need to be filled.

"Hmm?" She's prompting me.

"Yes..." Oh god, *yes*, I *feel* like a slut.

"Yes what?" She's going to make me say it.

"I'm a slut, Daddy." Why does it feel so much dirtier to say it out loud? "I'm *your* slut, Daddy."

With a muffled curse, she fists her hand in my hair and fills my mouth with the thick length of her tongue, kissing me ruthlessly, aggressively, taking possession of my mouth with a skill and hunger that demands my submission and I give it willingly, whole-heartedly, winding my arms around her neck, pressing my breasts against her chest, my hips rising and falling against her almost of their own accord.

"That's it, babydoll," she whispers between kisses, licking my lips, biting them gently, "grind your pussy onto Daddy's cock. Show Daddy what a slut his little girl is."

I do moan then, and she steals the sound with her kiss, stroking her tongue against mine as I do what she's asked, grinding my pussy against her cock, the thin material of her trousers and the scrap of fabric that is my thong the only things separating our bodies in this room filled with people.

And they're there, these other people, on the edges of my mind, their moans and whispered sighs mingling with the music that fills the room, and it turns me on all the more, imagining these Daddies and bois with their rock-hard cocks and these girls with their hungry wet pussies.

"Hey, all you cats and dolls," a bouncer drifts through, mellow voice rising just above the music, "let's keep the petting PG, okay? Above the clothes, folks. Everybody copacetic?" There's a smattering of sound that could be taken for assent, and the bouncer moves on, satisfied that she's done her job.

"Hear that, babydoll?" Jay whispers against my mouth, "Daddy can't touch that sweet little pussy of yours." I make a tiny mewling sound of discontent.

"Mmm...I know, baby," she strokes her hand down my back, "but I bet you can come without me touching you at all, can't you? I bet you can come just by rubbing your pussy against Daddy's cock."

I'm halfway there already, my clit hard and throbbing, the scent of my arousal rising in the air around us. I put my hands on Jay's shoulders for leverage and press my sex more tightly against her, grinding my clit against her hardness, her grip on my hips and the way she thrusts up against me telling me that the base of her dick is hitting her clit just right.

"I'm gonna come, Daddy, please can I come?" I whisper it in her ear, knowing without being told that I've got to ask, that I've got to have her permission.

"Do it, baby." Her voice is tight with arousal. "Come for me now." That's all that I need to push me over the edge, and I'm coming hard all over her, my pussy heaving and contracting against the bulge in her trousers, soaking the material as I shudder against her.

"That's it, babydoll," Jay's voice is still tight, her hands restless on my back and on my ass, "such a good girl, coming so pretty for Daddy. But you've got me so damn hard it hurts, and I'm going to need to feel that sweet little mouth of yours wrapped around my cock."

"But, Daddy, the bouncer said—"

"I know what she said." Jay cuts me off abruptly and plants my feet unceremoniously on the floor, rising quickly and scanning the room.

"Come on, babydoll." She takes my hand and pulls me behind her, back through the bar area, where the tempo of the music has picked up and the dance floor is filled with femmes and their fellas happily fumbling their way through the Charleston in the warmth of the burnt orange glow. Jay doesn't pause, though, cutting through the crowd efficiently en route to a single door at the back of the room, a door that would open onto a back patio in warmer months than this.

The air outside is cool but comfortable, and Jay takes us deeper still into the night, flipping the latch on the patio's back exit and leading us into the alleyway beyond.

"Down."

It's all she says, but I'm already there, on my knees, unfastening her trousers, unzipping her fly, breathing in her musk and the leather as her hand grips her cock, pulling it free and thrusting it deep into my waiting mouth.

It's too far, that first thrust, and I gag, I can't help it. I grip her thighs tightly to steady myself, never letting her fall from my mouth, taking control of the pace so that she groans and fists a hand in my hair, the other still wrapped around the base of her cock.

"That's good, baby girl." Jay's voice is a little unfocused, her head tipped back with pleasure. "You suck Daddy's cock so nice..."

Her voice trails off as I moan around her cock, and I know she feels the vibrations; I can almost feel her swell and thicken in my mouth. I suck her harder, my cheeks hollowed out, and replace her hand with my own, jerking her with my fist in unison with the steady rise and fall of my mouth, knowing she's close, knowing she can't hold out much longer.

"Fucking slut—" She wrenches my head back off her cock, pulling me upright, and I cry out, as much from the pain as from the sudden absence of her cock and the fear I've done something to displease her.

But then her hands are on my skin, beneath my dress, pushing it up above my hips as she turns me away from her, pulling my thong aside and bending me forward, my palms cool on the brick wall in front of me, bracing me as her cock nudges against the tight circle of my asshole.

"No, Daddy!" I cry out, genuinely scared. "Not there— nobody's ever done that to me there!"

Jay stifles a curse and edges her cock lower so that it slides wetly into my pussy. I cry out, a low keening sound; she feels so good inside me, and soon I've got her rhythm, fast and deep, her fingers bruising my hips she's holding me so tight.

"You'd better not be lying to me," she growls.

"No, Daddy—I swear!"

"Nobody's ever fucked you here?" She presses a finger to my asshole, teasing my opening, sending sensation flooding through me.

"No, Daddy—nobody!" Her finger sinks deeper, inching into me, stretching my virgin hole, and the dual sensations—her cock in my pussy and her finger in my ass—have me spiraling toward orgasm almost before I can gasp:

"Please, Daddy!"

"Come for me, baby." She's pumping me now, fucking my holes, breath hot on my neck, and then we're there, falling over the edge together, her hoarse shout echoing my cry of release as pleasure explodes through her body and into mine.

We stay like that for a minute or so, slowing our breathing and the rapid beating of our hearts, the muted sounds of the music drifting on the night air. Jay withdraws from me gently.

"Be a good girl," she says, stroking my hair, guiding me down. I circle the base of her cock with my hand and take her tenderly into my mouth, cleaning her with my tongue, taking time to learn the shape and texture of her, caressing her without the urgency that guided our earlier endeavors. When I'm finished, she tucks her cock back in her trousers and fastens the button, then draws me up into her embrace for a kiss that is long and sensual.

"Mmm…" Jay's sound of contentment warms me—it's a sound I could get used to, though I don't want to jump ahead.

"You are something else, Evie." She sighs. "Makes me wish I was in town more than once a month." Disappointment crashes through me, and I can't hide my expression.

"Hey now—" She forces my chin up so I have to look her in the eyes. "All that means is that you're going to have to cross those pretty little legs of yours good and tight until Daddy's back in town."

"Do you mean it?"

She nods. "I won't tolerate any other boys sniffing around you. Can you handle that?"

"Oh, Daddy!" I throw my arms around her neck, kissing her jaw, her lips, anywhere I can reach. "I'll be a good girl, Daddy— you'll see!"

"I know, babydoll." Her hands roam my back, then cup my ass possessively. "And in the meantime," she whispers in my ear, "I want you to go buy a set of plugs, and I want you to tease that tight little asshole of yours, make it ready for Daddy. Because the next time I see you? It's mine."

WINNER
TAKE ALL

Andrea Dale

Okay, contestants, listen up," the DJ said. "We start in five minutes, at eight a.m. sharp. Remember, one hand has to be on the vehicle at all times—your whole palm and fingers. You can switch hands as long as one is fully on the car. Except for during the fifteen-minute breaks, one every two hours, which I'll announce. You may not kneel, sit, lean, blah blah blah."

He didn't really say "Blah blah blah." I just tuned him out. I knew the rules by heart. I'd been *prepping* for this contest.

Yeah, it's tacky and stupid, the whole "keep your hand on the car longer than anyone else and win it" schtick, but the fact was, this truck would be a godsend for the nonprofit I managed. Even if I didn't win, the publicity would help tremendously.

But I was here to win.

I stretched, bending over till my palms touched the ground (thank you, yoga classes) and continued to size up my opponents.

I'd placed myself between the two people I thought would be

least competitive. One was a nebbish-looking guy, on the thin side, who kept nervously pushing up his glasses. I was banking on him forgetting and pushing up his glasses with the hand that was supposed to be on the truck.

On my other side, a pretty, petite blonde. For the life of me, I couldn't imagine why she'd want or need a truck. She didn't look the type to step foot in a truck. She was wearing painted-on jeans—probably designer, but I wouldn't know designer jeans if they were cupping my own ass—and low-heeled gray boots. Her makeup was impeccable, her big blue eyes made wider by the judicious use of mascara and her luscious lips glossed a lickable red. I suspected she didn't usually wear jeans; she looked like the type to wear little skirts and high heels.

Nothing wrong with that, if that was your thing. I certainly enjoyed looking at pretty women in little skirts and high heels, and fantasizing about getting up under those little skirts and seeing what kind of panties they were wearing—or not.

I'm not a skirt-wearing type of girl myself, and today was no exception. I'd dressed for comfort: jeans, sure, but broken-in, soft ones that wouldn't constrict movement; sneakers with gel insoles for extra support; and a T-shirt advertising my nonprofit.

"What's the Kensington Bird Sanctuary?" the blonde asked maybe ten minutes after we'd gotten started. She had a light, breathy voice, which suited her. Her dangly silver earrings caught in the light as she cocked her head at me.

"It's a rehab facility for birds of prey," I said. "I'm the manager. We could really use this truck to transport injured raptors to our facility."

Her laugh tinkled. "Oh, see, that's not fair," she protested with a little pout. "You're trying to get me to sympathize with you, and lose."

I shook my head. "Not at all," I said, and it was true. She'd asked, after all. "I just automatically try to drum up support. It's the curse of running a nonprofit."

"All right, then." She favored me with a dazzling smile, even white teeth and juicy lips. "I'm Grace, by the way."

"Teddie," I said, waving my free hand.

"Nice to meet you," she said. "*Very* nice to meet you." Her voice went a little lower then, and I swear I saw her look me up and down and up again. She delicately bit her lip.

Was she flirting with me? Really? I couldn't imagine it, but it still gave me a little tingle. I cleared my throat. "Ditto."

She asked me a bit more about the sanctuary, and I learned she was a buyer for a chain of fashion boutiques. The more we talked, the more I realized for all her cuteness and little-girl voice, Grace was smart and accomplished.

After a while, though, I was feeling antsy, so I put my other hand flat on the truck, pulled off my first hand, and turned around. I made nice with the nebbish guy for a few minutes, but he wasn't all that into chatting.

The first contestant to call it quits did so after the first break. One down, eight to go, and the truck would be mine.

If I didn't get too distracted by Grace, that is.

Her shimmery gray top was cut kind of low, so if she moved just the right way your eye was drawn to her cleavage. Well, my eye, certainly, and the eye of the guy on the other side of her, for starters.

Over that she had on an open-knit shrug that tied just under her breasts, enhancing the view. The crimson matched her lipstick. Her outfit was simple, yet all pulled together—it really was an *outfit*, an ensemble, as opposed to some clothes she'd just thrown on that morning.

Me, I'd never gotten the hang of that. My idea of "layering" is throwing a hoodie on over my T-shirt when it gets chilly.

The guy on the other side of her started chatting her up. Big surprise.

She gently rebuffed him, her voice sweet, her smile brilliant.

He wasn't the type to take no for an answer.

"Look," she said finally. "You're not my type. *Really* not my type."

His final try.

"You want to win this thing?" Grace asked. "Then stop. Talking. To. Me. Because if you don't, I'm calling the ref over here to say you're harassing me, and who do you think he'll believe?"

The guy retreated, but I barely noticed. I'd heard something unexpected in her voice. A steeliness.

At first I thought I imagined it; it didn't fit with her breathy voice.

My rational brain might have insisted that I imagined it, but my body clearly heard it—and reacted to it.

Right down in my three-for-five-dollar cotton panties.

Grace turned and flashed me her dazzling smile. "It's all about psychology," she said. "The psychology of getting people to do what you want. It's about figuring out what *they* want. Putting your hand on a car for hours and hours, just to win it? It's like a psychological form of bondage. Being told, *Don't move*," and her voice got that steely undertone again, the one that made my inner muscles clench.

I straightened my back, like a new recruit snapping to attention...or a submissive posing for her mistress.

I heard Grace's breathy chuckle, and I knew she knew what I was thinking.

"Oh yes, just like that," she said. "Some folks like cuffs and ropes and shackles—need them, even—but others...others know *choice* is as good a restraint as anything. It's all about power, and most people think the top has power, but that's not true. The bottom does. The bottom *chooses* to submit. Holds her hands out for the cuffs. Presents her sweet ass for the spanking. Doesn't come until she's told to—or comes on command, anytime, anywhere."

My head reeled even as my nipples snapped to attention faster than my back had, and blood rushed to my groin, making me aware of my clit, my lips, the way my panties clung to my crotch.

That innocent, breathy voice coming out of that pretty little blond form.

Aren't dommes supposed to be tall, imperious, stern, and wear black leather? Not petite, angelic, smiling, and wearing ruffly colorful fashion?

Maybe that's why she was affecting me the way she was. She wasn't a cliché, wasn't someone who used the tired old props.

In other words, she didn't need a dungeon to be a domme.

The DJ called another scheduled time-out.

Argh.

The showroom had only one tiny ladies' room, but Grace and I were the only two women left. She let me use the bathroom first, which was nice, except...damn.

Damn if I didn't want to plunge my hand down into my jeans, into my cotton panties, and stroke away the slick, needy urge she'd raised in me. A few minutes of privacy, that was all I needed.

But I knew she was waiting outside. I knew she'd know what I'd been doing.

And somehow, I didn't want to disappoint her. It was crazy, I knew, and yet I also knew that if I got myself off, I'd be... disobeying, maybe?

Grace hadn't said a word about what I could or couldn't

do—and, indeed, we'd only just met, so who was she to give me orders anyway—but I instinctively understood what she expected of me, and I wasn't about to let her down.

No matter how desperately I wanted to. It was hard to pee, being this aroused, but somehow I managed. I staggered out of the restroom feeling flushed and desperately unfulfilled.

Grace gave me a stunning smile and a bottle of water, then headed into the bathroom.

She also patted me, ever so subtly, on the bottom as she sailed by. She didn't say a word, but I swear I heard "good girl" in my head.

The local TV station came to interview us, asking each of us why we'd entered the contest. The nebbish guy surprised me by saying he wanted to use it to pick up chicks. Of course I used the opportunity to talk about the sanctuary, how we relied on donations, how important this would be for us.

I somehow managed to not sound distracted. I'm a good public speaker and I could talk about the sanctuary for hours, but I also know how to distill it into a few pithy sound bites. Still, I could smell Grace's delicate perfume and was constantly aware of the throbbing wetness between my thighs.

Plus I was dying to hear her answer to the question.

She laughed, the sound a gentle and genuine delight. Even the camera guy instinctively smiled.

"Oh goodness," she said. "I just can't resist a challenge, you know?"

Then, as soon as the camera swung away, she winked at me, and I got the distinct impression that winning the truck wasn't really the challenge.

I was.

I squeezed my legs together and immediately regretted the action, since it just made me hyperaware of my sodden crotch, my aching clit, my empty pussy begging to be filled by beckoning fingers.

As the contest wore on, she continued talking, her light voice spewing filthier and filthier things pitched low enough for only me to hear. Of course, as the contest wore on, people dropped out, so the remaining contestants adjusted themselves with more space between each of us.

Except for Grace, who stayed close to me...and I, admittedly, made no attempt to move away from her.

Close behind me, she whispered, "What's your poison, Teddie? Restraint? Cuffs and ropes and shackles, even if they're not needed? Orgasm restriction or forced orgasms, over and over? Blindfolds and gags? Spanking, whipping, caning?"

Behind my eyes I envisioned everything she was saying. Grace coming toward me with silvery handcuffs and chains spilling from her small hands. Grace wearing a strap-on dildo, her slender hips rolling as she thrust into me. Grace standing over me, holding a paddle, raising her arm...

And, almost ridiculously, in all of the scenes, Grace's makeup was perfect. She would never, I knew, break a sweat. And her nail polish would match the leather of the harness she wore, burgundy or royal blue or purple.

My palm, where it lay against the truck, was slick with sweat—in fact, I could see my handprints all over, from all the times I'd switched hands. The small of my back was slick with sweat, too, and I knew I was flushed.

"Answer me, Teddie." Light and airy, laced with control and command.

"Yes," I blurted. "All of it. Whatever pleases you."

Without thinking, I started to turn, forgetting to put my other hand down before I started to lift my first hand.

"No!" Her hand shot out and pinned my wrist, keeping my

palm flat on the side of the truck. It was the first time, in this whole long day, that she'd touched me flesh to flesh. The sudden feel of her fingers encircling my wrist, restraining me, triggered the long, slow roll of a mini-orgasm, coiling in my belly and uncoiling in my cunt in a series of shivery spasms.

My knees almost buckled, but I caught myself. Then I almost jumped out of my skin at a shrill whistle behind me.

"No touching the other contestants!" the judge, a florid-faced auto executive, barked. "Number Four, you're disqualified."

Grace was Number Four.

I remembered to change hands appropriately, even though they were shaking from the remains of my orgasm. "No, it's okay, she wasn't trying to distract me or anything, she's fine—" I protested.

"Sorry, those are the rules," he said.

I thought about calling him an ass, but that wouldn't have looked good for the sanctuary, so I bit my tongue.

"It's okay," Grace said, with a dazzling, sweet smile that made the judge's shoulders untense, just a little. "He's right—I wasn't paying attention, and I broke the rules. She deserves the truck more than I do, anyway."

But before he could lead her away, she went on.

"Win this truck, Teddie," she said, in the same tone as if she were commanding, "Lick me until I come." She leaned in, ignoring the judge's frown. "If you do," she whispered, "I'll punish you. But if you don't…"

She shook her head, and then she was gone, leaving me with a whiff of her perfume and a final sharp tremor in my clit.

And I knew if I was the last person standing with a hand on the truck, I'd win a hell of a lot more than the contest.

IT'S SO
PEACEFUL
OUT HERE

Elaine Miller

Mary's wife Gabriela caught an early-fall case of the sniffles, and Jo's girl Rainforest had to go help her hippie parents bring in a marijuana crop in a last-minute kind of way, and Beth's fuck-buddy Lyn suddenly needed to help her other lover move house, and everyone else was currently single, and that's how my Frankie ended up being the only femme on a camping trip with seven brotherly butches.

Now, don't get me wrong. We're an equal-opportunity bunch of dykes. It was kind of an accident that the seven of us had done a butch-bonding thing during a company campout almost a decade ago while working for an organization that ran women's shelters, and kind of an accident that we'd decided to get together the next year and do a just-us-dykes campout. But that was so much fun that the year after that was no accident, and it had become a tradition to grab tents, sleeping bags, and—when they were up for it—our lovers, partners, and girlfriends, and hit the back country once every fall.

Frankie is a handful at the best of times, with her tangled mass of dark curls being the most tame part of her sweet and bratty self. We'd been together four years, and I'd never been bored once. However, sometimes this tired old daddy found herself wishing for a trifle less spark, and never so much as on this trip. My Frankie is a natural appreciator of the butch breed, and something in her just kind of got worked up being the sole girly-girl in the midst of all us kinda traditional butches. She became stubbornly convinced that the only way we'd all survive camping was if we were each teased and flirted at until we were so distracted that we didn't know which end of the sleeping bag to get into.

At this point I have to interrupt myself again to state that I ain't a particularly possessive sort, and Frankie's flirting didn't bother me on that account. It was more that I knew my friends well, and while Mary was so happily married and monogamous that nothing would faze her, Beth and Lyn currently were having a tumultuous go of being polyamorous, and Beth could catch hell if the weekend's pics showed Frankie hanging around her neck. Chris was trying out the male pronoun for the first time this year, was considering the big change, and so was a bit jumpy about his sexuality, and Morgan was the most painfully shy butch creature I had ever met, and would blush right 'round the back of her neck at the merest sidelong glance from Frankie's sly eyes. If I didn't keep Frankie out of her lap, Morgan'd probably burst a blood vessel. All in all, I saw that it'd be my job to keep my brat under some semblance of control for what was going to be quite a long weekend.

In the end, though, it was I who made the whole problem worse. The nicest camping spot in the area was a certain small clearing surrounded in dense brush. It was a tight fit for all our various tents, but we'd decided that since most of our time was going to be outside the campsite we could just all squish in. Trouble was, if I could hear Chris in the far tent snoring well enough to know whether he was sleeping on his back or his side, that was not enough privacy for me. I'm as shy around my sexuality as my girl is bold, and as a result, apart from a little silent necking on Friday night, we hadn't had sex.

By Saturday afternoon, despite the busy day of hiking and similar group-style woodland adventures, the multitude of butches around wore at Frankie's self-control like she was a cat surrounded by toms, and she took to flirting with the no-contact rule—and with the other women—by squeezing by us on the trails, claiming that she just had to see this tree or this butterfly. When she wasn't cooing at Morgan, she was making eyes at Beth or bent over tying her shoes in front of one of the others, enjoying her femme power as each butch reacted in some way to her pestering.

Saturday at dusk, it all came to a head. Beth and Mary and I had gone off to enjoy an after-dinner stroll in the woods, it having been our turn to cook, and therefore everyone else's turn to clean up—including Frankie, who had sulked her way through food prep and had therefore been reassigned to the tidying team. We three butches stayed out for a half hour, sharing a cigar and a companionable silence as we watched the sun drop toward the horizon from a nearby hillside and then made our way back to camp, careful of our footing in the fast-dimming light. Someone had stoked up the campfire, and it was a cheerfully crackling beacon as we ducked and wove through the overgrown trail. In an anticipatory kind of way, I thought of the ice chest containing some fine Canadian microbrews and felt that all was right with my world.

When we arrived it was obvious that something wasn't right. It wasn't just the uncomfortable silence of my four in-camp butch friends. It wasn't the fact that Morgan was blushing so hard that even the firelight's rosy glow couldn't mask it. It was the sound, holy hannah, the familiar sound of my Frankie warming up to a really good orgasm. She wasn't even trying to be quiet about jerking off. The mood she'd been in, I suppose I was lucky she'd bothered to go into our tent and close the flap.

I avoided the eyes of my mates as I hurried across the clearing, intent on addressing the problem before Frankie came. Brats learn better if the bad behavior isn't self-rewarding. I unzipped the tent flap and dove inside. Frankie's startled eyes flew open and her thighs snapped closed, trapping her doubtless slippery little hand between.

"All right, you little bugger, I'm going to teach you about discretion," I snarled. "You've been the most exhibitionistic monster all weekend, and now you've made the other campers feel worried, exasperated, or uncomfortably overstimulated. And you've made me plain mad."

Frankie looked worried. "But, Daddy, I needed..."

"Shut up. That is literally the last fucking word I'll hear from you until I tell you you can speak again, you understand me? Agree by nodding or shaking your head, because one peep, syllable, or even an audible breath out of your pretty mouth and we're packing up and driving all night to get home, where you'll find out just how angry you've made me. I don't even want to hear you plump your pillow. The only sound you're allowed to make is your safeword."

Frankie just nodded, wide-eyed and silent.

"You've got a lesson coming right now!" I said as I pulled her arm roughly so she tumbled across my lap, making a conscientious effort to land silently. Well-behaved at last. Face-down, she turned inquiring eyes at me over her shoulder, and with an erotic charge, I noticed that she lacked entirely the sly, flirty expression she usually wore while her rounded ass was turned up to my hand. So I pinched her. Hard.

Frankie stiffened, visibly controlling her squeal, managing a silent exhale instead. She hated pinching—but it was a silent torture, and so I did it again, roughly grabbing the tender skin on the inside of her thigh, high up near her cunt. Her expression turned pleading as she struggled, but my brat was keeping her head at last, as she was silent still, and even struggled softly so as not to create a ruckus.

I lowered my voice. "You're going to be the most discreet little slut for miles, you are. No one is going to hear or suspect a thing. Our friends will leave us alone in here, and your punishment will go on until I decide you're done," I said, punctuating each final word with a pinch. Frankie's mouth opened in a silent pant. I tumbled her off my lap, and she landed in a ball on her back on our mussed-up sleeping bags, arms up to cover her breasts, her expression uncertain.

The nearby campfire shone brightly through the thin white walls of my tent, and I paused to admire my beautiful girl in the golden light. She had taken my breath away since the very first moment I met her, and none of that awe I felt had lessened with time. Of course, I kept a stern frown on my face. Frankie was such a dedicated brat that she'd be disappointed if I went soft on her before we got to her punishment.

The frown must have worked, as her eyes sought mine as I rummaged in my bag for my kit of toys. I hadn't brought much, what with my own shyness around sex and my wish to pack light for camping, but I'd still brought a few items. Just the necessities. Some clamps and cords, some nasty straps, a bottle of lube, one tiny bottle of nastiness I'd been saving up for just such an occasion, and of course, Daddy's dick.

"Sit up straight and put your hands behind your back," I

said, under my breath but striving to keep the edge in it. "It'll be no simple spanking for you. That makes too much noise. I'm gonna show you how to not be noticed, girl."

Frankie, perfectly in position, merely watched me carefully as I pulled the nipple clamps out of the bag. They were the kind that got tighter when there was a pulling kind of tension on them, which Frankie well knew. As I placed the clamps, which cruelly pinched her nipples, a tiny frown wrinkle appeared between her brows. That frown grew more serious as I tied a long lace through the end of each and tossed the ends over her shoulders.

"Roll over and get your ass in the air," I said flatly. "No, not like that. Up on your knees. Get on your elbows." This last change in position rewarded me with the sound of Frankie's extraordinarily quiet intake of breath when her breasts swung forward and the clamps dug in slightly. I pretended I hadn't heard a thing.

My girl twisted around as much as she could without chancing being punished for being out of position, and resumed watching me, her eyes eloquent with uncertainty, pleading, and a definite recurring heat. That I'd entered the tent and inter- rupted her jerk-off session meant she wasn't going to need a warm-up, so I progressed quickly to the more painful part of the lesson.

The next thing out of the bag of tricks was a collection of tiny, colorful, toothed clips meant for holding tiny locks of hair. With little interlocking fingers, these minuscule clamps were hell on the tender spots, so I placed them high up on Frankie's sweet inner cunt lips, starting right beside her clit. It was slip- pery going, and my fingers were drenched before I was done, so I leaned forward and thrust them into Frankie's mouth to be cleaned. Her eyes went wide and then fluttered closed as she suckled my fingers hard. Each strong pull of suction from my girl's hot mouth made my clit buzz and my cunt clench, and I was shocked to feel how hot I'd become in such a short time. I'd been so occupied with Frankie that I hadn't stopped to pay attention to my own intense arousal.

Fingers damp with spit but no longer so slippery, I went back to my pleasant task. Another row of tiny, maddening clips decorated her outer lips before I was done. I took care to keep them bunched forward; I didn't want to make the next step impossible. Frankie held her position, but kept twitching irritably, and her frown was steady now. Her gaze still held mine in between winces, so I knew she was doing fine.

"Such a good brat you are, now," I whispered "Get your ass a little higher, and put your head down."

Frankie obediently arched her back and dropped her forehead to her folded arms. Her sweet cunt pooched out at me, slick and pink and bristling with agonizing little clamps. She looked inviting, and I wanted her very, very badly.

So I took her. I peeled off my clothes, strapped my dick on over my own wet cunt and hard, buzzing clit, and knelt behind my slowly squirming girl. I squirted a generous glob of lube into my hand, pumped my dick a few times, and aiming carefully past the rows of tiny clamps, I slid a few inches inside my girl.

Her head came up abruptly, her whole body vibrating with tension. Her barely audible breathing took on a desperate air. My Frankie likes to scream, you see. I planned on testing her resolve. She knew I'd keep my word—that if she made a sound I'd pack up and take her home—and she'd be doing her damndest to not let that happen.

I wiped my lube-coated right hand on some discarded piece of clothing, held Frankie's hips, and leaned into her, slowly sliding deeper, listening to her breathing hitch as she struggled to process all the sensations, and holding back my own excitement. Not quite time yet.

"Baby girl, hand me those strings you've got attached to your nipples," I said with a smile in my voice.

Frankie understood all too well what I was about, and her fingers trembled slightly as she turned first left, then right to put the strings in my hands. I took up the tension on the strings over her shoulders, pulling painfully on her nipples, and her glance was full of reproach. I pumped ever so gently in and out of her cunt a few times and then settled into a slightly faster rhythm, never quite pushing all the way inside her. Frankie likes my cock deep, so I knew that I was adding to her frustration with the annoying clamps and the tugging on her tender nipples and the quick, shallow fucking.

Still silent, Frankie's expression had grown stormy, and her over-the-shoulder glares were frequent. I was enjoying myself hugely. To get off I need to fuck hard, so I could keep up this gentle teasing fuck all night—but I knew the clamps would need to come off soon, and I knew exactly how I wanted to ramp up Frankie's punishment.

I grabbed the lube bottle and spread a little extra on the base of my cock as I continued my fast, gentle thrusting and then I reached for the toy bag and took out one delightful little item. I'd never used this with Frankie before, so I hoped it would have a most interesting effect on her.

Her head down and her face covered in her own untidy curls, Frankie couldn't see what I was doing. Exactly three, oops, four or five drops of peppermint extract on my still-slippery right thumb set the stage. I grabbed both strings with my left hand, pulled back sharply, and as Frankie's head lifted again and her butt pushed back toward me, I slid my lubed-up and peppermint-covered thumb into her tightly puckered asshole. And then I started to fuck her hard.

Her breath stopped entirely; I could tell it was the only way she could keep quiet. But her body spasmed as the cold burn started, and she started to buck, unable to decide whether to respond to the fucking, the burning, the pinching, or the tug on her nipples. The burning won out, it seemed, as she suddenly flopped down on her belly, and my thumb slid out of her ass as my cock sprang free of her cunt. There wasn't a safeword to be heard, however, so I climbed on top of her sweet body and stuffed my dick inside her cunt again, holding her down roughly, the way she liked it; the way I liked it. I fucked her slow and deep and hard, without a sound except our harsh breath, panting in unison. I didn't last long. I came hard inside her, biting Frankie's shoulder as I did, so I wouldn't cry out.

Mindful of the torture the clamps had to be by now, I pulled out much sooner than I usually would and rolled my girl over to face me. Frankie was lovely, flushed, panting silently, hands held protectively over her clamped breasts.

"Daddy, may I come?" she mouthed clearly and inaudibly. "Please?"

"Finish jerking off for me, girl. But here's what you've got for lube." I said, looking into her horrified eyes as I picked up her delicate right hand and put six drops of peppermint extract onto the tips of her fingers.

She didn't last long either. Despite the inevitable burst of heat from the mint, despite the awful bite of the clamps, despite me tugging hard at her nipples, or perhaps because of all those things, she came so fast she could hold her breath through the whole thing, even while coming so hard her back arched, her hips bucked up, and she balanced for a moment on her heels and the back of her head, fingers quivering on her hard clit.

Peppermint drops only burn for a few minutes, so by the time I'd taken all Frankie's clamps off as she hissed softly with pain, the remaining sensation was gone. She'd been a very brave girl through it all, so I felt especially proud of her, and rather softhearted.

"You can make noise again if you want, baby girl," I said. "I feel like you've taken the lesson in discretion to heart."

Her giggle was a welcome first sound after all her silence.

"Daddy, you're mean," she said with a soft smile, snuggling into my arm. "You're a real brute. And you should bring me some water."

"Right away, my princess brat," I said.

I pulled on a T-shirt and my shorts, which I didn't bother to do up, slid into my flip-flops, and left the tent. Before I grabbed the canteen, I needed to pee something awful. I stepped away from the firelight, a few paces into the dimly lit brush, and almost immediately stumbled over Mary, who was oddly sitting next to Jo. And Chris. And Morgan. And Beth. Well, hell, Anne-Marie and Miko were here too. They were lined up like a butch shooting gallery, sitting in silence and darkness just outside our campsite.

"Um, guys? What the fuck?" I said, unaccountably stage-whispering the words while clutching the waistband of my shorts so they didn't drop like my jaw had.

I was faced with a row of silent, slightly abashed-looking friends. Then Beth, always the boldest of our brotherhood, pointed behind me. "That's what we were doing," she said, sotto voce.

I turned and looked, and there sat my light summer tent, beautifully backlit by a campfire generously built to burn almost as bright and hot as the sweet girl inside. Frankie, sitting up on the bed of sleeping bags and pulling tangles out of her unruly curls, was displayed in silhouette so perfect that I could see the points of her nipples outlined as she shifted, her arms raised to her hair. Her dark shadow shimmered in time with the golden, leaping flames beyond, and it was such a beautiful sight that the full import didn't hit me for a long, distracted moment.

Slowly and silently, I turned back to my dimly lit friends, who peered at me like guilty little boys, unable to make out the expression on my ominously backlit face. Morgan, the shyest of us, lost it first and started to giggle nervously. Then I couldn't hold it in any longer and roared with laughter. Everyone else followed suit, hooting with an obvious sense of relief.

"You pervy fuckers! You've been watching us the whole time! And I thought I was being so discreet!"

"We just knew that Frankie wouldn't mind..." Mary began before sputtering off into laughter again.

"Daddy?" said Frankie, her tousled head poking from the tent flap. "What's going on?"

"C'mere, my beautiful, exhibitionistic girl. I do believe you have an audience of butches with a confession to make to you. And then we'll see whether we need to do an encore."

MANCHESTER, 2000

Stella Sandberg

An arse tightly wrapped in a short silver skirt and perched on top of a pair of naked legs, pale on the verge of blue in the December cold, was walking in front of me. Not exactly what you'd expect to see on the pavement in the middle of winter. Then again, perhaps in England it is. People don't dress very sensibly here; it's as if they seriously believe the "mild" island climate means you can't freeze your nuts off. Not that she had any, despite the sequined dress worthy of a queen. The petite, curvaceous brunette with her long, straight hair let down was unmistakably female.

She had a friend too, a blonde, but I didn't pay much attention to her. I'm ashamed to admit it, but I was positively entranced by the buttocks moving in front of me, making the silver sequins sparkle with every step.

"Oh my god, the bus!" the owner of the buttocks suddenly cried out, and made a futile attempt to outrun it on her stiletto heels.

I hadn't planned on catching the bus, but I heard myself promise: "I'll hold it for you."

Oh well, I guess being crammed on a bus sweating in my new tan wool coat and missing out on the refreshing walk I'd planned was the least I could do in return for being served the spectacle of that magnificent bottom. In the trousers and dress shoes I wore, catching up with the bus halting at the bus stop down the street was child's play. I told the driver to wait and got the last window seat.

Before I knew it, I was wrapped in an almost indecently sensual perfume, newly released by body heat. The sequined femme was beside me, her friend across the aisle.

"Awfully sweet of you to hold the bus," she said, flushed and breathing heavily after her high-heeled marathon.

"Oh it was nothing," I said, "I couldn't have you kill yourself, trying to run in those shoes. I'm impressed, by the way."

I babble like that when I'm nervous. Upon closer inspection, her front turned out to be as good as her back. She was a formidable English rose, pale and freckled with delicate features and large hazel eyes.

She shrugged and laughed: "Practice. I'm Katie. What's your name?"

"Toby," I said.

Now that wasn't quite true, but my real name is long and girlish and doesn't go with my suit. I use Toby sometimes when I desperately pick someone up at closing time and don't want to be tracked down. Not that this was that kind of situation at all. I thought "femme" in my head, but the bird beside me was unmistakably straight. I didn't have a chance in hell, but at least she didn't giggle and say it was a strange name for a girl.

Instead she said: "Where are you headed?"

"Um," I said, partly because having her so close to me made

me unable to speak coherently, and partly because I had no idea.

This wasn't even my bus. The best thing I could do was probably to get off at the next stop and walk back for a bit, before it went too far in the wrong direction. But of course I didn't want to get off now. I quickly decided to ride until Katie got off, even if that meant the end of the line. I'd be late for Liz's New Year's party, but I didn't want to go anyway, knowing the scene was so small up to three or four of my exes might turn up. That, and a whole bunch of one-night stands. Riding this bus next to a gorgeous straight chick was probably the most fun I was going to have tonight.

"Don't tell me this isn't your bus?" Katie said.

She was reading my mind. Either that or my awkward behaviour.

"Did you hear that, Anne?" she said to the blonde. "He got on the bus just for us!"

He. She'd said *he.* That explained her lack of surprise when I introduced myself as Toby. Well, I do pass occasionally, but my face is boyish rather than manly, and most of the time the contrast with my mature style of dress makes people suspicious. My voice tends to be a giveaway too, but I'd caught the flu a couple of weeks before and still had that sexy, husky voice.

"Aw," Anne said disinterestedly.

"Why don't you come with us?" Katie said. "We're going to this huge party, glitz and glamour, and we're allowed to bring a date, but as you can see we don't have any."

She named the biggest, poshest nightclub in town and eyed my tie: "You're dressed for the occasion. But of course, stupid of me, you already have plans!"

I shrugged. "Not really. No *better* plans anyway."

"You're coming, then?" she said.

"Yeah," I said. "Thanks for the invitation."

I wondered if she was used to chatting up strange men on public transport—or what she assumed were men. She seemed slightly tipsy, not enough to do anything nutty, but perhaps she was just being polite. Perhaps she'd "accidentally" lose me in the crowd as soon as we got inside the club.

I wondered a lot of things. Why they hadn't taken a cab, why two gorgeous girls didn't have male company to a New Year's Eve party, if what was really happening was that I'd interfered with a femme couple.

After chatting with them for a while in the club, I was firmly convinced they were straight, though. Straight and slightly naïve. Younger than me, twenty five-ish, though I guessed I looked their age as a man. A couple of perfectly normal party girls on a big night out.

It didn't take long before Anne had company too. Unlike Katie, she'd chosen to put emphasis on her cleavage, and she definitely had one to put emphasis on. I guess cleavage gets more attention in a crowded club than buttocks, no matter how impressive the buttocks. They're sort of the wrong height to notice. Like I said, Anne was a blonde too, and blond hair seems to draw men like bees to honey. Soon she had several fellows competing for the privilege of buying her drinks. Katie just had me, so I guess I did a good job looking intimidating. Or perhaps it was the way *she* looked at *me* that made the geezers give up before even trying.

Now I'm the first to admit I think I'm quite a looker, as far as butches go. But as far as men go? Perhaps she fancied my style, my tailored suit and expensive new coat. Well, I am stylish. But I'm working class and I don't exactly pretend anything else. Perhaps my masquerade was good enough for her, though. At least it was better than hers. I'd immediately pinned her down as a working-class bird with a decent job and chances of climbing, playing at being "refined" but forgetting as soon as she had a good enough time. That short, skin-tight, sequined dress sort of gave her away too, even though she looked stunning in it.

I couldn't believe those large, light hazel eyes were looking at me in a way that left no room for doubt. Looking *up* at me, because she was just tiny enough to be shorter than me in stilettos. At some point, perhaps to steer her out of the way of some drunkard, I'd put my arm around her and let it stay there. She didn't seem to mind. In fact, she seemed to wait for my next move. The whole concept of flirting while passing, or passing while flirting, freaked me out, but it also turned me on. And I was going to have a good time tonight, damn right I would!

I bent down—just a little, I'm not *that* tall—and kissed her pink rosebud lips. She kissed me back in a way that wasn't exactly "sophisticated." It turned me on immensely, and I wondered if she'd done too much social climbing to follow me to the loo. I figured probably not, from the way she pressed herself up against me. I let my hands slide down over those lovely sequined buttocks just to make sure. Nope, she wouldn't mind.

"Follow me," I mumbled into her hair.

She got it at once and eagerly let me lead her by her cute little hand.

There was a queue at the ladies', of course. Also, I sometimes have ladies screaming at me when I enter innocently just to pee. If I entered with a woman and locked us up in a stall, someone would probably go fetch security, just to be a pain in the arse. This wasn't exactly the kind of club where anything goes. So I left Katie in the queue and went to check out the gents'. Of course you had to pass the urinals to get to the stalls, but the lads were dashing in and out and I figured I might be able to sneak in Katie. Also, blokes were less likely to fetch security just because some fellow got lucky. As long as I passed it should be fine. I didn't want to think about what might happen if I didn't.

I managed to sneak Katie in okay, and to my relief, the stall was clean and spacious. I'm not squeamish but I have limits, and if the loo had been anything like the urinals outside, I'd have darted right out again, hot sex or not. Luckily the lads seemed to have left it alone for most of the evening.

We kissed again and she started messing with my collar and tie. I decided I could afford to let her unbutton one button. It was a risk, she might notice the lack of Adam's apple or brush against my breasts, which are just a little too perky to pass as muscles if you get too closely acquainted with them. But I couldn't resist. Having her drunken hands fumble to get me undressed made me even wetter than I was before.

Enough is enough, though. I couldn't have her freaking out on me *now*. So when she'd managed the one button I turned her around and pressed my groin to her buttocks. Yeah, I was packing. What? It was bleeding New Year's Eve, and some of the one-night stands I'd figured bumping into might fancy a second night. Anyway, I couldn't be caught unprepared. I'd tied down my most discreet dildo to my thigh. Katie would have to think I was pretty poorly equipped—so what? It's not the size, it's what you do with it, et cetera.

She seemed impressed enough with the bulge in my pants, panting and rubbing her arse against it. I took the time to feel that glorious arse of hers and then slid my hand in between her thighs. I was not the only one to be soaking wet. I'd almost expected her to be the no-knickers kind of girl, but she did have some ridiculous string of lace disappearing between her plump buttocks. I promptly disposed of the offending thing and felt her up properly. She was ready and willing and able, all right, and almost seemed confused I'd bothered to stick my hand in first. All right then, if that's how straight girls liked it, I would play my part.

The sound of my zipper made her whimper with anticipation. I quickly took out my cock and stuck it up before she got the idea to look back or something. I normally adhere to some standards of sexual hygiene and use a condom, but this time I was just too hot and bothered to give a damn. I couldn't risk the delay. I'd have to boil my cock when I got home, but I take a certain wicked delight in doing that anyway.

I started thrusting my hips, which made her moan. She was so wet the dildo almost felt too small, slipping around in her uncontrollably. But like I said, I know my stuff. I held her hips a little tighter to keep her from thrashing about too much with excitement and made sure it reached the right spots. She moaned louder and louder. The sound of her and the feeling of slipping my cock in and out of her wetness made my clit ache for release. Luckily, being at the giving end of a strap-on is usually enough for me, and this time I was so randy I'd get off in no time.

Just as I came I realised I'd have to do it discreetly, or she'd wonder at my ability to go on. I clenched my teeth and almost suppressed a guttural sound. Then I thrust into her with renewed energy and groaned some more to cover it up. Somehow the idea of having to conceal even my orgasms made me even hotter and I came a couple of times more in quick succession. By now she'd probably just figured I was the loud kind of bloke. If she even noticed, she was so busy making noise herself. Her moans had peaked into what was almost yelps. I hoped she was on the verge because I was getting real weak in the knees.

She was. As soon as I rubbed her clit with my thumb she arched her back and pressed her behind up against me, pushing at the wall in front of her and screaming at the top of her lungs. I tell you I was stunned. At first I almost thought something was wrong, she got a cramp or something. Then I just went with it and surprised myself by coming spontaneously, without taking command over my climax. I did come to my senses quickly enough to take advantage of her having momentarily lost hers, though. Hurriedly I wiped down my cock with a paper towel and stashed it back into my pants. Then I pulled down Katie's skirt with a last look at those round, white buttocks.

I couldn't just leave her in the gents', something might happen to her there, so I led her outside. A guy at the urinal clapped his hands ironically and a couple of others hooted. Katie was still dizzy from the orgasm, and possibly from hyperventilating, and leant heavily against me. Frankly, she smelt like pussy. I probably did too. I wondered if I should try to find Anne, but after a glance at my wristwatch told me we'd missed midnight while we were in the loo, I figured she might well have gone home with one of her admirers. It was easier to just put Katie in a cab. The glimpse I caught when she got into the passenger seat reminded me her sorry excuse for panties was flung in a corner somewhere. I leaned over and put a hand on her naked thigh.

"Remember to keep your knees together when you get out of the cab, love," I whispered in her ear.

That seemed to turn her on and she dragged me down by my tie and kissed me fiercely. The cab driver sighed and drummed his fingers against the wheel. For a moment I was afraid she'd ask me to get inside the cab with her, or call her tomorrow, or give her my card, or something else I'd have to decline. But she was a wise girl, a fun-loving girl, and did nothing of the sort. I watched the cab drive off and felt my clit pounding with remembrance.

I think she knew. A dildo doesn't feel *that* much like a cock—not that I'd know!—and I didn't buy her *that* many drinks. I think she pretended not to know, even to herself, to give herself license to engage in the adventure without having to go through some identity crisis. Or perhaps she was more cunning than that, perhaps she pretended just for me, because she thought that was the way I wanted it. Or perhaps it simply turned her on. I'll never know for sure, and for sure I'll never forget her.

GOOD GIRL, BAD GIRL

Sinclair Sexsmith

I.

Sometimes, I am a Bad Daddy: I hate it.

I hate it and I want it and I crave it and I hate that I want and crave it, this, this girl, this way that I use her, this way she uses me. Sometimes I resent it. Her, me, my own desires. Why do they run this way? Where did these wounds come from, or are they scars now?

I have to remind myself not to ask myself too many of those questions. That it's okay to want what I want. That after the flash of feminist guilt, as Karlyn Lotney once wrote, it is quite the handy little fetish.

And it is a fetish, or maybe rather it is many fetishes wrapped up and tied with a big, pretty red satin bow. Power. Gender. Age.

I hate it, but I have never loved any play more.

This is what happens.

I sit on the couch reading a book and drinking tea after the dinner she made. For me. She finishes the dishes, brings her book out too, sits next to me. I don't watch her as I take another sip of my tea. This is what I practice: Not paying attention. But in not paying attention I still pay attention, I just don't let her know that I'm paying attention. When I notice I'm focused on her, I try to turn the focus inward. What do *I* want right now? And I feel something stir.

She inches closer to me. I turn a page. She sighs inaudibly. I turn my eyes to the pages of my book, move them along the words, not reading.

"Daddy?"

I don't look up, yet. "Yes?"

"May I sit on your lap, please?" It comes out in one quick string.

I pull the bookmark out of the back of the book and slide it between the pages, close the book, set it on the coffee table, look up at her. Her eyes gleam gently. Hopefully. Her dress is pushed up from how her legs are crossed on the couch and I can see a hint of her inner thigh. I breathe in. Keep it under control.

"Yes, sure, darling." With the Good Daddy voice.

She climbs over, sits sideways on my lap, knees bent over my thighs. Wraps her arms around my shoulders and buries her face into my neck and collarbone. Her hair is soft and thin and smells clean and faintly sweet, and I bring one hand up to the back of her head, play with the gentle curls there.

She settles in and drops a hand to my chest, resting it on my waist. I shift a little, a growl rising in my belly. My arms fold easily around her.

"Daddy?"

"Yes, darling."

"I like to sit on your lap." She snuggles a little closer. I can feel a tightness spreading in my groin. I don't say anything. "Do you like it?"

"Yes, darling."

"Does it feel good?" Her voice drops softer.

"Yes."

"Does it feel good..." She's whispering now. "In your pants?"

I stir. My cock stirs, jumps. The growl grows. My arms tingle and tense, a sensation I want to let out with a fist. "Yes." I whisper too. Our mouths are close.

I am a Bad Daddy. I want my girl to do dirty things; I want to do dirty things to her. I know she'd let me if only I asked, but sometimes the desperation is more fun. The arguing with myself. The attempts at holding myself noble, resisting her sweet girlish body. Feeling dirty for wanting it so much that my palms ache.

"I feel you getting hard, Daddy." She keeps her head low, shifts her hips to rock against my cock. My eyes roll back, wrists go slack. So soon. Fuck.

"Do you, now."

"Yes." She waits. "Can I feel it?"

"You want to?"

"Yes." Again, a pause. "Please?"

My hands flex. "Please what?"

"Please can—may I touch your cock, Daddy?" She knows how I like to hear it. All the way through, from the "please" to the way she should address me when we play.

I try not to groan audibly. "Well, since you asked so nice and pretty. Yes, sweet girl, you may."

She bites her lips and shifts her hips again, reaches down with one hand to grip the hard packer I'd slipped in after dinner. She strokes it through my trousers.

"Daddy." She presses close to me, hand still stroking. "It's too big. It should come out of your pants, Daddy." Her lips are nearly touching my ear and she knows how I love that. My whole body shudders, relaxes, stomach muscles clench for a moment as I contract and release. I picture her pretty hands with her perfect sparkly red nails wrapped around my cock. I am a Bad Daddy, and she is so good.

"It's big and hard in your pants, Daddy. Don't you want to take it out? It's too tight under there. Too big. Can I take it out? Daddy, can I?" Her lips are on my neck, earlobe, jaw. I can barely see straight.

I breathe out. "Yes. Yes, you may."

She slips off my lap and crouches between my knees, staying on her tiptoes on the floor, and unbuttons, unzips my pants, pulls the too-big cock from under my briefs and straightens it out, poking from my fly. She wraps one hand around it, then the other. "Mmm." She hums a little, smiling.

She watches her fingers stroking my cock for a quick minute, then looks up at me, still crouched. "Daddy..." I bring one hand down to her jawline and trace it gently with my thumb. She leans into it a little, eyelids half-closed.

"Daddy," she says. "I could put my mouth on it. Don't you like that? You like it when I do that. And I like to make you feel good. Can I?"

I stiffen, feel my cock jump. Breathe in. It is so dirty to want this so badly. To hear her ask over and over at each step of the way. I fight every urge I have to just shove my cock into her mouth, slide it over her tongue, and instead do my best to resist, and the tension keeps my body cocked and loaded.

She flattens her tongue and runs it over the very tip, smiling up at me. "I'm a good girl, Daddy. I know how to make it feel good."

That breaks me. I breathe out. "Yes, I know you do, sweet girl. Put your mouth on it for me."

She swallows the spit she is already excessively producing and opens her mouth, and that momentary flash of a pause burns my eyes, her hovering open lips just centimeters away and closing in.

When she drops down, my cock slides in effortlessly. Mouth open, lips wet, she pauses to say quietly, "I like it in my mouth," then bends her neck again and takes it deeper, sucking expertly.

I could watch her do this for an hour, two. What is it about this that gets me so hard and hot? I can't feel it, but I can *feel* it, every stroke, every graze of her teeth, every swirl of her tongue. My hips tighten and knees rotate open, just barely, pushing.

"That feels good," I manage to mumble, vision blurry, as I slide my hand into her hair, tangle my fingers into it.

She glows at the slightest praise. "You like that, Daddy? Does it make your cock feel good to be in my mouth?"

"Yes, darling."

"I like it, Daddy. You can put it in my mouth when it gets big and hard. It feels good. I like to suck on it."

"You're getting it all wet."

"Yes, Daddy. My mouth gets wet when I suck on it. Want to see?"

I nod. She swallows a little again, pools the saliva on her tongue, dips her neck down to my cock and slides it deep, far back into her throat. I groan. She leaves it there for as many seconds as she can. When she opens her mouth to slide it out, it glistens slick with the thick spit from her throat. She smiles as it strings from the tip of my cock to her lips.

I groan again. "Baby, that's so good, you're so good at that."

She rubs her lips together, licks them, swallows. Shifts her legs and raises up to bring her mouth close to mine. I quickly bring my hands to her waist, squeeze the sweet curve of her hips, and bring her body in closer and bring her mouth to mine, kiss her hard. I'm practically panting.

"I like it. It feels good for me too. See, Daddy?" She raises one knee up next to my thigh on the couch and pulls my hand from her body down between her legs, and I feel her pussy against my hand, swollen and slick, before she slides two of my fingers into her easily.

"Feel that? Sucking on your big cock makes my pussy all wet." Her mouth is by my ear again. "It's okay, Daddy. You can put your cock in all my little holes. You like it when we play this game. Want to put it in my pussy now, Daddy?" My fingers go in and out, pausing to rub circles over her clit. "See how wet my pussy is? It's wet for your cock, Daddy. So it will slide right in and go in and out. Don't you want it in there? I want you to put it in, I want you to, Daddy..."

She shifts in my lap and, knees on either side of my thighs, starts guiding my cock toward her hole. I watch, slip my fingers out, bring my eyes up to her face as she reaches for the shaft to guide it in. "Do it," I growl low, already thick and pulsing just feeling her slick lips touch the tip. "Slide it in, baby. That's good. Yeah, like that." And she does, she slides it right inside, slow, and pushes all the way down until her thighs are pressed against mine.

We both shudder and sigh, and she rests her cheek on my shoulder for a second before clenching her thighs and lifting her body up and off me until only the tip of my cock is touching her opening, then pressing down and letting her weight rest on me again, clenching, squeezing her thighs together.

My eyes roll back. I breathe in. I can't stand it.

"I like it, Daddy. I like it going in and out. I like your big cock in my little pussy. Does it feel good, Daddy?"

I move my hands to her hips and hold her steady, start thrusting with my hips. I'm close. She's got me so close. "So good, you're such a good girl, baby, my good girl." My lips can barely form words. She kisses me, sucks my tongue into her mouth, wraps her arms around my neck and squeezes me tight with her thighs and cunt.

"Do it more, Daddy. Do it harder. Please? Please put it in my pussy. Please, harder, Daddy, please, please…" She knows I'm close from the way my hips are shuddering, faster now, more of a shake than a thrust. She keeps her lips next to my ear. "Do it, Daddy, come in my pussy, make your cock come in my pussy, Daddy, please, come, Daddy, come…" And I do, I thrust harder up inside her and my groans and grunts turn into yelling, *fuck, yeah, fuck*, body pulsing, gushing, until I feel every drop squeezed out of me, and I collapse back, head rolling gently, eyes closed, as she kisses my neck and rocks gently against me.

I breathe out. Open my eyes. Smooth her hair, run my hand along the side of her body. "My good girl."

She grins and brings her mouth down to mine again, sweet soft kisses, and I wrap my arms around her.

II.

She is a bad girl.

There is very specific protocol if she wants me to fuck her. She is supposed to ask for it, nicely. If she's embarrassed, she is to sit on my lap and tell me she has a secret.

She wants it, all the time. She is the first girl I've dated seriously who has a higher sex drive than I do.

I want her to own her desires. To know there's nothing wrong or shameful about wanting to be fucked, to be opened, to be taken. But sometimes, she can't. She forgets she's supposed to ask, and instead drops hints and tries to turn me on, to entice me. Sometimes, this frustrates me. Sometimes, it becomes a game, reminding her she is a bad girl for wanting it and not being able to tell me.

This is what happens.

I sit on the couch reading a book and drinking tea after the dinner she made. For me. She brings her book out too, sits next to me. She doesn't look at me as she finds the place marked by a small piece of paper and starts reading. I'm not paying attention; she's watching me from the corner of her eye. Her legs stir, she shifts position, pulls them underneath her as she inches closer to me.

I turn a page. She turns her eyes to the pages of her book, moves them along the words, not reading. She's tried to get my attention all through dinner. Touched her foot to my ankle under the table. Gazed at me, lusty and devourous. Touched my hand and forearm, leaned across the table to display her breasts. Kept her thighs apart.

She gets frustrated that I'm not paying attention. Starts pouting a little. She sighs, audibly.

I ignore her.

We read a while. I'm deeply involved in the middle of this book, and besides, didn't she just get fucked this morning? I am impatient with this seduction routine, it makes me feel anxious, itchy. And simultaneously, something dark in me growls from down low.

I finish my tea, put my book down, and get up to piss. When I emerge, she watches me from the couch, waiting for some cue from me, and almost rolls her eyes when I give her none. She sets her book down on the coffee table a little harder than necessary and gets up to prepare for bed.

We cross next to each other in the hallway and I slam her up against the wall, face first. She whimpers, gasps. Breathes in.

"Is this what you wanted?" I grip her arm and twist it behind her, my mouth close to her cheek.

She hesitates. "N-no," she starts.

I twist a little more. "Isn't it? You need some attention, pretty girl? Need to get touched, played with?"

"No, no, Daddy, I just—"

"You just what?"

"I just...wanted you to kiss me, Daddy. I wanted to be close to you."

"And?" I wait. She hesitates. "What else?"

"I wanted..."

"You wanted to get fucked, didn't you."

Her body pulses and I feel it. "Yes," she whispers.

"You're supposed to tell me when you want to get fucked."

"I know, Daddy."

"You know?"

"Yes, Daddy. I'm supposed to tell you my secret. I'm supposed to sit on your lap and tell you I have a secret. I'm supposed to tell you. I'm sorry, Daddy!"

"That's better." I stroke her hair. She's on edge, knows she's in trouble. "You're behaving like a bad girl tonight, keeping your legs open and coming on to me. I bet you're already wet, aren't you."

She twitches. She knows she is. I bring my other hand down between her legs and push her wet panties aside, slip my finger between her pussy lips. "See?" I whisper. "Bad girl."

"No, Daddy."

"No? No what?"

"No, I'm a good girl, Daddy. I'm good!"

"Oh you are, huh? Do good girls get all wet like this? Hmm?"

"No, Daddy," she whimpers.

"No, I didn't think so. You're a bad girl tonight. And you

know what Daddies do to bad girls?"

She tenses, and heat flushes to her cunt and cheeks. "What?"

I release her from the wall and shove her back toward the bedroom door. "Let's find out. Go," I say, low and hard.

She turns when she gets into the bedroom, leans a little against our tall bed, keeps her mouth shut. I unbuckle my belt and we both hear the metal-against-metal clinking sound. I see her chest shudder, mouth water, a Pavlovian response. She breathes out.

I pull the belt from the loops in one fluid motion. "Bend over the bed."

I see a flash of fear in her eyes; she doesn't like pain too much, and she doesn't like the belt. Some nights, I care about that. Not tonight. Tonight she's going to get used, because I am a Good Daddy and that's what she wants, even if she doesn't quite know it yet.

I push her panties down over her thighs and they puddle around her ankles. I start out slow, with sweet little slaps against her ass cheeks, warming her up. She's on edge, tender and nervous and sensitive, jumping at every touch. I will be gentle, kind of.

"This is what bad girls get," I hiss in her ear as I start hitting harder.

She whimpers. Breathes in, and her chest heaves.

"You've been a bad girl tonight. Haven't you?" I keep the blows steady, increasing force and speed just a little.

"N-no, Daddy, I'm a good girl." She's tearing up already. This will be quick.

"You wanted to get fucked tonight, didn't you, bad girl?"

"Yes, Daddy."

"And did you tell me that?"

"No, Daddy."

"What are you supposed to do, when you want to get fucked, bad girl?"

"To tell you my secret, Daddy. I'm supposed to tell you. That I want to...get fucked."

"That's right." I let the belt drop but hang on to it and smooth her ass with my hand. She gulps air, wipes her teary cheeks on the bedspread. "That's right, you're my bad girl tonight." I pick up the belt again, let a few more blows fly. Her ass is getting red, I can see it flush even in the dim light of the nightstand lamp. "I get to play with you how I like. Isn't that how it works?"

I run my hand along her ass again, dip my finger between her legs. She's dripping onto her thighs. I lean over her body so she can feel me close to her.

She whimpers, manages to whisper through her tears, "Okay, Daddy."

"Good. Now, five more, then I'm going to get my cock out." She's trying not to cry. "Count."

I back off and roll my shoulders to prepare, push the skirt of her dress higher up on her waist. I fling the belt and the edge of it catches her ass, leaving a sharp mark.

She gasps. "One."

"Good." I hit her again, a little lighter.

"Two." She whimpers. "Three."

She's squirming. I press her back into the bed. "Four! Daddy!" She can't take much more.

"You can take it," I growl in her ear. "One more. For me. Because you're a bad girl."

She sobs a little, scrunches up her pretty face. I lift my hand and prepare the belt. "Spread your legs," I say, and she does, just a little more.

"That's my girl," I soothe, and she relaxes, just a little more. I let the last blow snake from my hand, the whole length of the belt over both cheeks.

"Five!" she yells into the mattress as another sob escapes. She's trying to be strong and take it, I can tell, but she's still scared of the pain. "Shh, shh," I whisper, bending over her body as I run my hands along her ass, striped hot red. "You okay?"

"Yes, Daddy."

"Good." I stand and let the belt drop to the floor. I unbutton, unzip my jeans, pull them and my briefs down and off, and retrieve my cock, pull the harness on, and tighten the buckle. I leave my T-shirt and binder on.

"Stand up, and take your dress off." She does and pulls it over her head, tosses it to the floor, shivers as the air touches her skin. I run my hands along her body, pinching her nipples and cupping her tits, then push her back onto the bed, gently but with force, and she lets me. She breathes in. I knock her legs apart at the knee and she spreads her thighs. I grip my cock in my hand, lube it up from the pump bottle on the nightstand.

"Spread your pussy open for me."

She brings her fingers down, both hands, and pulls her lips apart so I can see her shiny pink slit split open. I push my cock inside, slick and easy.

She sighs. "Ohh."

"You like that? See, bad girl, you'll get fucked when I am good and ready to fuck you. You know how to ask nicely." I work my cock in and out of her. She pulls her thighs up, rocks her hips back to take it deeper. "And when you ask nicely, you get fucked nicely. But when you forget how to ask, you get used up. You understand?"

She grips the blanket with her fists, opens her eyes to say "Yes."

"I get to use you up. Fill up your holes, fuck you and take you how I like." I bring two fingers to her mouth and shove them in. "See how you get all filled up, bad girl. Filled in all your pretty little holes." I work my hips harder and she bucks against me. She's close: starting to turn her head from side to side, thrashing her body against me and the bed.

She mumbles against my fingers and pushes them out of her mouth to say, "Daddy, can I come? Please?"

I grin at her asking. "Oh, aren't you being good, asking me nice and pretty like that." I keep thrusting inside, harder. "Yes baby, go ahead and come." She moans and thrashes more, slamming her hand down on the bed and arching her back, squeezing so hard that she pushes my cock out and her legs straighten. She comes with a small gush and shudders, stomach squeezing, back arching, until she falls back and her body quiets, and she breathes out.

She catches my eye, reaches up for me. "My sweet Daddy," she murmurs.

"Dirty little bad girl. Did you like that?"

"Yes, Daddy. Thank you."

I bring my mouth down to hers again, sweet soft kisses, and she wraps her arms around me.

THE BUCKET LIST

Charlotte Dare

I knew I was in love with Ellie that morning in New York City as we sat together, bumping along in the back of an air-conditioned cab. It was a month after "the kiss" and she still wanted to be friends—a good sign. She smelled so good, clean and fresh from some Bath & Body Works lotion girly-girls wore and perpetually minty from constant refills of Mentos chewing gum. As she rambled about loving jaunts to the City, I realized everything I ever wanted was right beside me. I watched her shiny cranberry lips move as she spoke, but all I could think about was the kiss several weeks back, the number two item on my bucket list Ellie helped me cross off. Sweet and sensual, that kiss was still as palpable as if it had happened only a minute earlier.

When she finished praising New York for its culture and sophistication, she looked ahead at the snarled traffic and grimaced. "I don't know how people can live here."

"I couldn't do it," I said, still studying the curve of her soft face. Her delicate antique earrings danced from her lobes each time we hit a pothole.

"Stop staring at me," she growled with half a smile. "I hate it when you stare at me like that."

"I'm not staring," I said. "I'm just looking. Not my fault you're cute."

"Oh, yeah, right." Like always, she dismissed my compliment as though I were a used-car saleswoman on the last day of the quarter. "What time does the curtain go up?" She knew very well we had tickets for a two o'clock matinee of *Mamma Mia!*

Looking back, asking my unavailable friend if she wanted to be my Number Two was an extraordinarily stupid thing to do, but my attraction to Ellie since she and her partner bought the condo unit next to mine two years ago had become unmanageable by late spring. I was starting to say and do stupid things with alarming frequency.

I sneaked another peek at her profile as she kept her eyes peeled for every car and bus our driver nearly sideswiped along Forty-Second Street. Ellie was fifty-seven, but her smooth Mediterranean skin, Bambi brown eyes, and youthful enthusiasm made her ageless to me.

"Can I have a sip of your coffee?" she asked.

I handed her the cup and stuck my hand into a white paper bag containing the cinnamon streusel I'd bought earlier at Grand Central Station. I bit into the warm, moist cake and grinned at her, my lips coated with cinnamon sugar. "Wanna kiss me?" I asked, assuming she would laugh it off as innocent flirtation. To my surprise and hers, she leaned over and pressed her lips against mine, grinning back at me as she licked the sweet mixture from her lips.

"That's hot," I joked. Although I was playing it cool, that kiss sent a jolt of tingles through my entire body.

"I know," she confessed, reapplying her lipstick. "I've been thinking that since June."

I nearly choked on the streusel. "What do you mean?"

"What do you mean, *what do I mean?*" She grew flustered, trying to downplay her comment by picking lint off her black capri pants. "I told you I liked it right after it happened."

"I know you did, but I had no idea you've been thinking about it since June."

She rolled her eyes and turned toward her window.

I was more than shocked. I'd had a fantasy of being with an older woman since I was a teenager, but by thirty-eight, I had all but abandoned hope of it ever coming true. Ellie was older, beautiful, but in a relationship. I had considered myself lucky when she'd consented to the bucket list kiss that night on my balcony after a couple of glasses of Merlot.

"Ellie, are you trying to tell me something?" I gently patted my highlighted spikes to make sure they hadn't fallen victim to the humidity.

"Honestly, Suzanne, I don't know. I don't know what I'm saying. Did I enjoy the kiss? Yes. Do I want to kiss you again? Yes, but am I going to? No. I'm in a relationship, first of all, but I also really love our friendship and don't want to ruin it."

We got out of the cab at Forty-Sixth Street so we could grab a quick bite to eat before the show. We continued the discussion strolling up Broadway toward Rockefeller Center in the heavy air.

"Then why did you kiss me in June?" I asked after taking a few minutes to process the unreality of the conversation.

"I don't know," she snapped. "I thought it would be fun to be on your bucket list, something wild and silly. You know how I am. I never ever imagined it would actually turn me on." She shook her head. "And I'd keep thinking about it for weeks afterward. I've been with Cheryl for over fourteen years."

"You also said it's been a long time since things felt right."

She sighed heavily. "We've really been trying to make it work. She's been talking about retiring from the hospital and doing part-time, in-home care."

I remained quiet, rubbing at the last spot of streusel stickiness on my finger as we walked.

"Look, Suz, it's never gonna happen for us," she said. "So let's not talk about it anymore and just enjoy the afternoon together."

Her angst charged through me like I was a lightning rod. "You don't have to get all worked up about it. I'm sorry I kissed you in the cab. I promise I won't ever bring up the subject again."

She grabbed my arm and stopped before we approached a hot dog vendor. "You didn't kiss me in the cab. I kissed you. And I want to kiss you again. That's why I'm getting all worked up."

"Shit," I whispered to myself. I felt like a total schmuck for joking with her about my bucket list in the first place. She had a partner. What was I thinking? But then who ever thinks a fantasy is really going to come true?

I ordered us two dogs with the works, and we slapped each other's hands away as we both waved our money at the vendor. "Will you let me fucking pay for this?" Ellie said. "You get the cab back later."

She took a huge bite of her hot dog and absorbed the Manhattan skyline, intentionally avoiding eye contact.

After several minutes of silence, I said, "Ellie, can I be honest with you?"

She exhaled deeply. "Please do."

"I would love nothing more than to kiss you again. It's all I've been thinking about since it happened—a heck of a lot more than you, I'm sure. But our friendship means the world to me, and I don't want to ruin it either."

"This is so crazy. I'm nineteen years older than you. What do you even see in me?"

"It's probably the last thing you want to hear right now, but you're everything I want in a woman—I just love being with you. You're fun, sexy, so pretty, and most of all, you get me."

She smiled, her brown eyes sparkling above the rims of her DKNY shades. "But I'm not single."

"I know."

She grabbed my Diet Coke and sipped from my straw. "And too fucking old for you."

We laughed and, in unspoken agreement, savored the rest of our day in New York as friends, with no further mention of bucket lists or secret desires.

After our excursion to the city revealed more than we'd both intended, Ellie avoided me for a good two weeks—six days in New Hampshire visiting her daughter and grandson made it easy for her, but it made me a wreck thinking she'd washed her hands of the whole sordid situation. By the second week, I was missing her like crazy, convinced she was scheming to find a diplomatic way to end the friendship so I wouldn't go all Glenn Close on her ass. If it was true, I would survive, even though the thought of losing her as a friend crushed my heart. But I was a butch after all—I didn't chase down hot femmes, they chased me.

When Ellie finally texted *Found a great new Chardonnay*, I flew downtown to the gourmet shop for the perfect complements to her wine selection. Okay, so we would be friends and nothing more. Fine with me. As I prepared the bistro table on my deck with brie, horseradish cheddar, crackers, grapes, and citronella candles, my stomach fluttered. *Are you serious*, I thought. Butterflies, clammy palms? This wasn't a date—it was just Ellie and our regular Wednesday night wine tasting slash bitch fest.

The first glass of wine went down quickly and easily for both of us, no cheese chaser or fruit accompaniment, just straight down and into the bloodstream. A few sips from our second, and we were back into the familiar terrain of relaxed girl talk. As cool as I played it, inside I was dying. She looked more beautiful than ever, her cheeks shiny and bronzed from the sun.

"I hope you're not still feeling weird about New York," Ellie said. "I'm not."

"Neither am I."

Liars.

"Good," she said, her legs bobbing on the edge of the wrought iron bistro chair.

"So I bet Cheryl will be glad to give up these night shifts when she retires." The selfish bitch in me wondered how it would impact my time with Ellie.

She nibbled a slice of cheddar pensively. "She has seniority. She could've given them up a long time ago."

"Why didn't she?"

She gave me her famous *Duh* look. "Let's just say it was better for the relationship when we weren't together constantly."

"I can't imagine anyone not wanting to be with you constantly."

"You know how it is. You were with Angie for eleven years."

I studied her gorgeous, softly aging face and that sensual bottom lip I daydreamed of biting on numerous occasions. "And I knew things weren't right with us. That's why we're not together anymore."

"Well, you're young. You shouldn't stay in an unhappy relationship."

"But if you're old, you should?"

"I didn't say that, and I never said I was unhappy with Cheryl."

"You never said you're happy with her either."

"Suz, you're still so young. You don't understand."

I shook my head at her stubbornness and leaned back in my chair.

"I don't think I've ever been as happy as I am when I'm with you," she said quietly.

The butterflies returned in a swarm on that one. Maybe it was my empty-stomach wine buzz or just wishful thinking, but I swear I caught her checking out my chest as I stretched. Maybe she was just reading the Ed Hardy logo on my black tank top.

"These mosquitoes are terrible tonight," she said. "Should we go inside?"

"Sure, we can if you want." I downed the rest of my wine like a shot.

We got up in unison to gather the bottle, glasses, and snacks and take them into my living room. As she reached across me to grab the cheese knife, I stuck my nose in her hair and moaned at the sweet coconut scent of her shampoo.

"What are you doing?" she asked with a smirk.

"Nothing. What are *you* doing?" *Son of a bitch*, I thought. What the hell was wrong with me? My heart was racing just standing near her, and now we were heading to my couch. I followed her through the sliders, watching her ass as she went inside.

"I think you better slow down and eat something," she said over her shoulder.

"And ruin this nice buzz?"

We arranged the food and drink on the antique chest that doubled as my coffee table. I sat in a chair as Ellie curled up in the center of the couch. She shot me a look. "What are you doing over there? Afraid of me now?"

I giggled. "Why would I be afraid of you?"

"The dirty old lady says she wants to kiss you again and suddenly, you're sitting clear across the room."

I stood up and poured myself another glass, my hands shaking to match the rest of me. "As I recall, you said it's not going to happen again, so what difference does it make where I sit?"

"Fine." She pursed her lips and absently played with the strands of hair falling out of her hair clip. "Sit wherever the hell you want, but you better eat something. I think you're getting sloshed."

"Fine. I'll eat something." I plunked down next to her on the couch and made a pepperoni and cheese cracker sandwich, stuffing the whole thing in my mouth.

The setting sun burned red through my sliders. She gently bounced the edge of her wineglass off her lip as she returned my gaze, and I was jealous of the lipstick print her mouth left on the rim.

"Here, have some of these," Ellie said and shoved a few grapes in my mouth.

Her middle finger was warm as it brushed over my lips. I closed them around her finger for a second, expecting her to yank it back. She didn't. Instead, she slid it across my bottom lip and then tasted it.

My clit erupted into wild pulsations as we stared into each other's eyes, her breathing suddenly shallow and quicker. My mouth watered at the thought of tasting her tongue again, the sweetness of her full tits, her pussy as I would explore it slowly, gently with my mouth.

"Would you get mad at me if I kissed you?" I whispered, my lips inches from hers.

She smiled with her eyes, shook her head almost impercep-
tibly. I took her hand in mine and it was trembling. She looked
down, suddenly shy.

I leaned in and kissed her, gliding my lips across hers, lightly
flicking my tongue around her mouth. She moaned, scooped my
face in her hands, and kissed me harder, sucking my lips till I
tasted the fruit she'd eaten.

"Suz," she whispered through kisses. "I can't stop thinking
about you, and not just about kissing you. I can't fucking sleep
at night."

"What are you thinking?"

She didn't answer, but she didn't have to. I gently nudged
her back against the cushioned arm of my couch and slipped
my tongue deep into her mouth. She wrapped her legs around
my waist, her arms around my torso, and squeezed, digging her
fingers into my back.

"I keep thinking about you making love to me, and it makes
me so horny. I shouldn't be feeling this way, but I can't stop. I'm
such an awful person."

"I'm sorry, Ellie. Just tell me if you want me to stop."

"But I don't want you to," she whimpered.

I slipped my hand up her shirt and caressed her butter-
smooth side, running my hand over her pelvic bone and down
to her ass.

She was breathing hard, kissing me harder as my fingers
found her nipples poking up from her firm breasts. I twisted
them with my fingers as she devoured my lips, refusing to let go
of my face. Her tongue twirled around mine as my hand worked
its way into her pants, sliding over her bush and into her wet
pussy.

"Oh, my god," she moaned as I rubbed her swollen clit, slowly
up and down, savoring her slick velvet against my fingers. Her

legs opened wider, her body moved in rhythm with my hand as my fingers spread out across her pussy, some caressing her lips as my middle finger steadily worked her clit.

"Mmm, you're gonna make me come," she whispered, tightening the grip her arms had looped under my shoulders.

I stopped fingering her, intending to finish the job with my tongue, but she grabbed my hand and shoved my fingers back into her pussy. "No, don't stop. This feels so fucking good."

I pressed into her more firmly and stroked her slowly, all around, faster as she pumped her pelvis into my hand. She clung to me, panting in my ear, her climax building slowly, torturously until it rocketed her into orgasm.

"Oh, shit, Suz," she breathed. "Oh, god, that was so good. I can't believe it."

"I can't either," I said, kissing her gently on the forehead. "Maybe you'll sleep better tonight."

She exhaled deeply. "Or it's gonna be even worse." Snaking her arm around the back of my head, she pulled my mouth onto hers and licked my lips. "I wanna taste you so bad." She pushed me off her and back against the other sofa arm and was on me with the urgency of Cinderella at ten to midnight.

"Are you sure you want to—" Before I could finish the sentence, she ripped my cargo shorts and my black Calvins down to my ankles.

Her warm tongue on my throbbing clit was welcome relief as her hands roamed under my tank top, around my bare stomach, reached for my tits, pinching my nipples. After teasing me gently with her tongue, she found the spot and moved in for the kill, eating my pussy until I was shuddering in ecstasy.

We held each other until our bodies settled and then cuddled for what seemed like hours after. Ellie nuzzled up closer under my arm. "How did this happen?" she whispered.

I brushed her bangs out of her eyes. "I hope it happened because we both wanted it to."

She looked up at me and smiled, her beautiful brown eyes sleepy with satisfaction. "You certainly didn't force me." She sat up and began fixing her disheveled clothes. "It was a wonderful experience, but it won't happen again. I'm sorry." Glancing into the mirror behind the couch, she raked her fingers through her hair.

"You mean like the bucket list kiss?" I felt bad after I said that, but the determination in her voice stung.

"This is different, Suzanne."

"But I know you'd rather be with me."

She glared at me. "This isn't only about Cheryl. I'm almost twenty years older than you."

"That doesn't matter to me."

"It should. I had breast cancer."

"I know, and you survived."

"The point is it could come back. I'm almost fifty-eight years old. You're thirty-eight. I'd never put that on you."

"There are lots of people my own age who've had cancer. Should I not date them either?"

"Suz, you're not getting it. I'm too old for you, and I just couldn't leave Cheryl now. She's sixty-two years old. What's she supposed to do if I come home one night and say, 'Hey, guess what, I'm leaving you for someone twenty years younger'?"

Fearing my eyes couldn't contain the deluge of tears threatening to burst forth, I got up and switched on a light in the corner of the living room. "Thanks for killing the afterglow. Care for a bottled water?"

"No thanks. I should get going." She walked over to me and took my hand. "Suz, I really had an amazing time with you tonight—but I always have an amazing time with you. That's why we can't do this again."

I squeezed her hand. "I'm sorry if I did anything to make you feel uncomfortable."

"You didn't." She smiled as she studied my face for a moment. She said good night and leaned in for a gentle peck on my lips.

"Good night." I let her leave without incident despite my desire to throw my arms around her and beg her to leave Cheryl.

The days and weeks after our night of passion were torture. With all the preaching and proselytizing about how we couldn't ruin our friendship, we'd still managed to fuck it up thoroughly and in record time. No matter how hard I tried to forget Ellie, I just couldn't. Something about her made it impossible. But what could I do? She belonged to someone else. If I was destined to languish on Lonely Street for all eternity, it was a penance well deserved, but I knew I couldn't do it living next door to her for much longer.

Autumn came and went, and I was slowly going crazy alternately obsessing about Ellie and then browbeating myself for still wanting her.

On the Monday morning after New Year's, I crunched across the frozen parking lot, carrying the garbage to the Dumpster before work.

Ellie caught me as I headed to my car. "I saw the paper yesterday," she said.

"Happy new year to you, too." As much as I desperately wanted to drag her into my car and drive us far away, I opted for ambivalence, aided by bone-chilling air that kept my face naturally stoic.

"Why did you put your place on the market?" she asked, wrapping her arms around herself and rubbing them.

I stood my ground at my open car door. "Why does it matter

to you? You haven't spoken to me in months."

"Not to make an issue of it, but you haven't talked to me either."

"Not to make an issue of it," I mocked, "but you have a partner and made it abundantly clear that wasn't going to change."

"Well, it has—right before Christmas, as a matter of fact."

"What do you mean, you broke up with her?"

She hugged herself tighter against the cold. "I didn't have to. When Cheryl asked me why I never seemed happy anymore, I broke down—completely. She just knew."

"About us?"

Ellie shook her head. "That it was time to let go."

"How is she? Is she all right?"

"She will be, we both will."

"Well, if you ever want to talk over a glass of wine, friend to friend, let me know."

"Suz, I just can't be your friend."

Although I had made peace with our situation a while ago, hearing her say those words was like catching a snowball with my face.

"I can't be just your friend 'cause I'm in love with you," she continued. "I need us to be more. I've needed it since the first time you kissed me." A smile tickled the corner of her mouth.

The breath I'd been holding for months billowed out into the crystal air. "You should come over tonight. I have a great Riesling chilling."

Ellie smiled wide through chattering teeth.

"Plus, you might be interested in the new item I've added to my bucket list since we last spoke."

HAPPY ENDING

Rachel Kramer Bussel

Marisa smiled to herself as she welcomed her newest client, a woman who went by Em—at least, that was what she'd booked the massage appointment under. Marisa was lucky because for the most part, none of her clients turned her on the way the women she bedded did; but then again, none of them, in her three years as a massage therapist, had been butches like Em. She worked on the Upper West Side, a safe distance from her Lower East Side apartment, from the bars she frequented in Brooklyn where she would dance in a series of slips, or sometimes just one see-through one, that did little to conceal her very large breasts, the flowering tree tattooed on her back, or her desire to laugh and flirt and kiss and sometimes fuck, all right there, on the dance floor or in the bathroom.

She didn't like to take women home with her, though she was happy to go to their places on occasion. Her home felt too sacred for what invariably was a one- or two-, possibly three-night stand. Something always tended to fizzle with these budding passions, at least on the part of her partners; they saw her more closely and decided that another femme would suit their fancy, or couldn't handle her need to meditate and be alone for a few hours a day. Some of them balked at the fact that she couldn't see fit to adhere to strict roles, not after casting off the ones her mom had tried to push on her growing up. She didn't want to be a simpering wife, but nor did she want to be simply a submissive femme; those roles felt as constricting as any others. After so many years of these fly-by-night affairs, Marisa had resigned herself to getting what she wanted from her fantasies; maybe it was because she pushed too much, demanded too much, but was it really asking a lot for her to have a sexy, kinky, hot butch who'd let her get on top on occasion?

All those heated exchanges flashed through her mind as she prepared the soothing music, dimmed the lights, and welcomed Em into the room she considered her home away from home. In many ways, where she worked was her true home, because as much as she aimed for a New Age, Zen-like calm in her home, there was little to be done about the rumbling of the subway or the drunken screams late at night that often startled her from her calm. Her best friend, Candace, thought she needed to loosen up, but Marisa had her way of doing things, and at thirty, that was how she wanted them done. She couldn't control the strangers on the street or the MTA's schedule, but she could control what went on within the confines of the room she'd spent six days a week in for the past eight years.

She'd started out wanting to be an artist, but not only was she frightfully bad at the act of the hard sell, especially on the streets of SoHo pressed up against so many other struggling artists, it took some of the magic out of the act of creation. After a friend told her she'd become a massage therapist, she'd looked into and gotten hooked on the idea of pouring the energy she'd previously exerted onto canvas directly into other people's bodies. The high Marisa got from hearing someone moan in bliss as she dug and dug and dug deep into their backs, their necks, their arms, their legs, seeking the hidden treasures, often twisted and worried into almost unrecognizable shapes, from putting a smile on people's faces, from knowing that every single day she gave them a few minutes of pure pleasure, made her happier than she could remember being.

But this new client would be a challenge, she could tell, because after instructing Em to get fully undressed, she returned to the room to find the woman wearing a tank top, men's briefs that clung to her meaty thighs, and socks. "So, Em," she tried, placing a gentle hand on the woman's arm. "What brings you here today?" She let the CD player unleash the gentle classical music into the room and further dimmed the lights, taking one arm in her hand, trying to quell the current of very unprofessional energy she felt racing through her.

"My back. It's giving out. I was told by my chiropractor I had to start getting it worked on or I could really be in trouble."

"Well, this is a wonderful place to start. I just need you to relax," Marisa said, flopping Em's arm to get it to soften. But the woman wasn't used to relaxing, at least, not like this, and it was clear after ten minutes that Marisa's skills were going to be wasted if they didn't resolve this dilemma.

"Maybe you should turn over," she said, and Em, whose eyes were closed, grunted and begrudgingly obliged. Even in the dim light, Marisa could tell Em had a strong, fine back, the kind that would make her able to, say, lift a girl in her arms easily. Marisa had an urge to run her fingers through Em's spiky blond hair, but instead she spread the other woman out and let her hands drop down to her sides, then whispered, "It's okay, it's just me, relax." That alone didn't do it, but it brought them closer to a bodily truce, as Em let herself sink just a little bit more into the table, her body going limp, allowing Marisa's fingers, now warm with oil, to slip under the tank top and press into Em's shoulder blades.

She worked quietly, tempted to hum as she did when alone in her apartment, but not wanting to throw off the mood. Some clients loved to chat, to use her as an unofficial, and decidedly cheaper, therapist, while others used their massage time to zone out, to go to some deeper spiritual or mental space that they could only access within those four walls. Marisa was fine either way, and she too welcomed the silence, because it kept her free to play out the fantasy filling her head as she pressed her body weight against Em's.

She tried to dress modestly at work, wearing black or gray or sometimes white dresses or blouses and skirts that didn't show too much, settling for a pale lip gloss, mascara, and some dangly earrings to showcase her femininity. She suddenly longed to lean down, pull her breasts out of her bra, and press them against Em's back, to turn the woman over and tantalize her with them hanging ripe and full of promise before her.

Em had gone stiff when Marisa's hands roamed from her tense shoulder blades down her spine and were now working her lower back, dangerously close to her glutes. There was a reason they asked clients to get as close to naked as they could stand, and that was mainly so the therapists could have access to all the parts they needed. Most clients didn't realize until repeated visits that everything in the human body is connected, so getting a full head-to-toe massage, even though it was only the back that sang with pain, was more beneficial than simply localized pressure.

"Relax," Marisa whispered, this time a little closer to Em's ear than was strictly professional. Her lips might have brushed the other woman's skin; if they did, it happened so fast she hardly noticed, except that she got a faint whiff of cologne, enough to make her nostrils flare. Whatever the scent was, it was brisk, manly, sexy.

Marisa decided to skip Em's glutes and work her way from the bottom up, so she pushed the woman's legs apart and began with her feet. They were a little rough, but not utterly uncared for, though they were a far cry from her own, which received weekly pedicures and nightly applications of lotion. Marisa heard a noise as she pressed into Em's foot, and then it pressed back against her in protest. "That tickles," Em said, the first hint of mirth Marisa had noticed.

She put the foot down and started with the woman's calf, which was knotted, and clearly strong. "What do you do?" she asked, the question still within the bounds of the client/customer relationship, though Marisa had more intimate reasons for asking.

"I'm a tour guide, mostly upstate, Westchester, sometimes Jersey," Em said, flexing into Marisa's touch this time, rather than flinching away from it. "That feels good," she went on. "Lots of hills, plus I lift weights."

"Put your head back down," Marisa said gently and applied herself diligently to Em's calves, then knees, one by one, until she was at her thighs. She'd had no trouble working on all manner of models, actresses, and generally beautiful women, the kind who spent hours of upkeep on their appearance, who might have turned the heads of each other had they found one another outside the very chic and proper world in which they lived, but who Marisa saw as belonging far from her world. She'd made out with a femme or five, bedded one or two, even, but the women who made her heart pound, who made her catch her breath and go all coy and blushing, were butches. Always

butches. Beyond that she didn't have a single type; some were
tall and thin, debonair, almost, while others were stocky and
rough.

"How would you feel about me taking off your tank top?"
Marisa whispered, the tone of her voice possibly betraying her
interest. She wanted to touch this woman all over, to see her
come alive, to watch her melt, to give her back to herself.

Em opened her eyes and stared directly into Marisa's; they
were a fierce hazel, snapping and sizzling. "Are you asking as a
masseuse or as a woman?" she said.

"A woman," Marisa said. There was no point in lying when
she was getting so aroused. "Look, I know this might not be
your usual thing, and I've never done this before with a client.
But I want to make you feel good. I want to give you a happy
ending." She cursed herself for her babbling the minute the
words were out; *Happy ending*? Really? What a stupid phrase.
It belonged in fairy tales, but as a sexual act it was ludicrous. *I
want to make you come on my fingers*, she could've said. *I want
to make you wet*. Anything else.

But Em forgave her verbal faux pas and took Marisa's hand,
sliding it up to her breast. "One of the other reasons my friends
wanted me to come here is for the sheer pleasure of being touched.
My girlfriend of twelve years left me last year and I kept the apartment, the bed, the art. It looks just like when she left, except she's
moved on, and I haven't. It's hard for me to let people touch me,"
she said, and Marisa knew it wasn't just a butch thing, though
she'd been with her share of stone butches and had gotten used
to that separation of body and desire, of control and want; they
gave to her in other ways, many other ways.

"Do you want me to?" Marisa asked, leaning down to lick
gently along Em's firm belly. "I'd like to. No one has to know.
I like to give pleasure," she said, and realized it was true, both

on the job and off. She had always loved going down on women much more than having them between her legs; there was something about the act of touching a woman so intimately that filled her with a kind of joy she couldn't get any other way.

"Yes," Em said, her eyes now closed, her voice a bit strained, and Marisa saw the pride she had to let go of in order to let Marisa in. "Yes, please touch me."

Marisa stared at Em, the older woman's face relaxed now, for perhaps the first time since their session had started. "Beautiful" was the word she thought of, though of course she could never say it. Beauty was reserved for womanly women, for curves and lips and breasts and glamour, but this butch was beautiful, no doubt about it. How could Marisa not see beauty as she eased up the tank top and revealed large, natural breasts, weighty with need? She leaned down and sucked one nipple into her mouth, feeling it harden against her touch. She stroked her tongue back and forth over it, enjoying the sensation as her other hand wandered wherever she wanted: along Em's cheek, down the back of her neck, along her arm.

Marisa wasn't much for kink, the kind with whips and chains, but power play like this, getting Em to give herself over, to surrender to the kind of pleasure she'd been denying herself? That was a power trip Marisa was glad to take, and take she did, sucking on the other nipple while letting her hand edge between Em's legs. The woman balked at first, tightening her thighs around Marisa's probing fingers, and Marisa retreated, recognizing the silent dance they were doing. She moved downward, massaging Em's feet until the woman moaned, really digging into the ball of each foot with her knuckles, pulling on the toes, showing her the power her hands held, their mastery, their knowledge.

She continued with the massage in an almost-normal way,

stroking Em's face gently, though she couldn't resist tracing her small lips, relishing the feel of her tongue poking out. Marisa had sucked many women's cocks, but she still loved the way her index finger looked sinking between Em's lips. "Are you ready for me yet? Are you ready for me to touch you there, to make you come? I hope so, but you can't call out, you have to stay quiet. Can you do that for me?"

Marisa was giving Em a challenge she was sure the woman wouldn't refuse; her pride and her arousal would be too great. In the dark, there was no one watching them, no one who would tell her secrets, and Marisa felt Em relax as she said, "Yes," and this time, meant it. When Marisa reached for Em's underwear, Em lifted her hips and let her remove them. She smiled to herself when she saw the merest hint of pale fuzz on Em's pussy. Em waxed or shaved, even though she was the only one touching herself. Marisa liked that, and showed Em how much she liked it by stroking upward along her wet slit until she found the pearl not-so-hidden between her legs. Em's clit was large and hard and the moment Marisa's fingers met it, Em pressed back against her and let out a small moan. "Shhh," Marisa warned her as she circled her clit, eager to get to know it.

But the warmth and wetness below beckoned, and Marisa sank two fingers into Em's pussy. This wasn't usually how things went; she was usually the one bending over and taking it, at least the first time. On her home turf, though, to have a woman spread out before her was a treat Marisa wanted to make sure to honor. She pressed her fingers fully inside Em while the palm of her other hand pressed gently above her sex, her thumb seeking out that powerful clit again. "Yeah, that's it," she whispered as Em started circling her hips to aid Marisa. Marisa felt Em's G-spot right away, practically leaping out at her, urging her on, guiding her fingers as much as Em's moans. Em, to her credit, kept her hands up and away, leaving Marisa to feel her way to ecstasy.

And it was ecstatic, Marisa realized, as she shut her eyes and moved strictly by feel, adding a third finger, knowing that in another time and place, she could add more, could fill Em with all kinds of toys and delights. For now, her fingers were more than enough as she pressed Em down against the massage table and gave her the most intimate massage of all, her fingers coaxing and pressing and twisting and turning. Em was so close, and the ferociousness she felt inside her was at odds with the calm music pouring out of the CD player. There was nothing calm or New Age about what she was doing to Em, nothing calm about her breathing—panting, by now—as Em bucked back against her, then sank down onto the table with relief and desire and need.

Marisa read Em's pussy the way a palm reader looks at a life line, divining exactly where she was most needed, taking away, she hoped, some of Em's pain and putting in its place only pleasure, only wetness, as she felt her inner walls tighten around her, giving her back some of what she was giving. It was that circle of pleasure that filled Marisa with what felt like an otherworldly kind of bliss as Em went over, seizing Marisa and coming against her fingers. She did open her eyes then, did look at Em, who, through slightly filmy eyes, dared to look back. If they were anywhere else, Marisa would've kept going, would've given Em more, would've sunk a finger into her asshole while she was on her hands and knees, would've licked her clit while her fingers got crushed and soaked.

But their formal time was almost up, and they both knew it. Marisa washed her hands, then got a warm washcloth to soothe Em's sex. She put that in the hamper and then got Emma on her stomach and used her special oils to give an abbreviated version of her usual massage, still feeling the echo of Em's pussy pulsing against her fingers. "I want to do so much more," Marisa whispered in Em's ear, empowered by the darkness, by the sense of being in charge that her "office" gave her. "I want to stroke your ass and press my thumb there while I slide a big metal cock into your pussy." Marisa had never spoken like that on the job before, and had rarely even been tempted to think such thoughts.

Hearing Em's moan of encouragement spurred her on, and she used their last few minutes to spin a tale that involved fucking Em in every hole, in covering her with chocolate, then licking it all off. "Oh god," Em said, her verbal responses minimal, but her body thrusting up against Marisa's hands. When the buzzer rang, Marisa cleaned Em off, then helped her put her clothes back on, a ritual clients usually performed themselves.

When Em went to tip her, Marisa pushed it back into her hand. "Save it and take me to dinner this weekend," she said. "Dress up in a suit. I'll wear something hot. Then you can be the one to finger me under the table." Their fingers entwined, the bills tickling Marisa's palm, as Em leaned forward and, for the first time during their encounter, kissed Marisa, sucking on her bottom lip, then sliding her tongue into her mouth. She cupped Marisa's ass, leaving it tingling as she walked out the door. *The happy ending is just the beginning*, Marisa thought as she readied the space for her next client.

TAMALES

Kathleen Bradean

Christmas spices stung my eyes and made them water. My mouth watered too for the red New Mexico chilies and green pasillas that perfumed our tiny apartment kitchen. Beside the pot of red sauce was the pork shoulder, slow cooked until it fell from the bone. On the back burner, a speckled black steamer waited for the corn husk bundles we would make later.

Kerri slouched at our tiny kitchen table as she read the paper. Her coffee mug hovered between the table and her lips, forgotten as she leaned forward to concentrate on an article. She set down the mug and slid her hand over her gelled black hair. The second she realized what she'd done, she folded the paper and sighed.

"Ay, Papi, and you worked so hard to get that curl to drape just right. *Qué lástima!*" I said.

Her eyes narrowed. "Smart-ass."

"Better a smart ass than a dumb-ass."

I stuck out my tongue at her.

When she rose from the table, I squealed and ducked behind

the refrigerator door. She didn't come after me. With a touch of a pout, I peered around the door. She checked her reflection in the microwave door and tugged down a lock of her bangs.

"It's a forelock, not a curl."

I slipped my hands up her shirt as I hugged her from behind. She dressed like a *chulo*, but on her, it was hot. It wasn't as if she tried to be a boi. She just was one.

I kissed the nape of her neck and let go. "I have masa to grind." I shoved her lightly. "Go soak the corn husks."

Instead of leaving the kitchen, she lifted the lids on the pots. "Yum." She closed her eyes as she inhaled. A cloud of scented steam engulfed her.

Standing at the sink, I rubbed husks off the hominy. The dried corn had cooked with *cal* the night before and then was left to soak until the morning. It was a ton of work making the masa from scratch that way. Mama bought freshly ground masa from the bodega. Even my *abuelas* thought it was too much trouble to grind it by hand, but I did it from scratch. Kerri called that "being more Mexican than thou," but she was the one who liked all organic food, and I couldn't find organic masa. Besides, home ground tasted better.

"Stay out of that sauce," I warned Kerri as she dipped pork shreds into the pungent brew.

She tasted it anyway, and then more. "It doesn't seem so hot at first, but then it builds." She took another bite. "Wow." She fanned her tongue.

My hands went onto my hips, balled into fists. "Serves you right. I told you to stay out of my pots."

"You look like your abuela Teresa when you do that. All you need is a wooden spoon to wave around." Her lips glowed as she licked the burn away.

Even though I knew that she was right, I scowled at her.

That probably made me look even more like my grandmother. My voice was like Mama's. When I laughed, I was Tía Julia. I loved that they were there with me even when they lived eight hundred miles away.

"I should take a wooden spoon to your butt," I said.

Kerri stepped close. "I'd like to see you try."

When she got quiet like that, I got good chills from my heart down to my clit. I struck a barrio-girl pose. "I would, but I don't have time to be messin' with you right now. Maybe later, if I got nothin' better to do." I gave her a long stare.

"Ooh, I love it when you act like a tough little chica."

It was a big act, one that I couldn't keep up. I tossed my hair back. "Don't tempt me. Now shoo! Get out of my kitchen. I have work to do."

I put the heavy metate on the floor of our narrow apartment kitchen. Abuela Teresa didn't use the short stone table anymore, but it took a lot of pleading to talk her into giving it to me. The way her crinkly hands caressed the surface, I understood it was like giving up her only link to her mother, but she knew that I was the only one in the family who would appreciate it.

The pocked surface of the metate was coated with several lifetimes of oils from seeds and chilies crushed on its surface. Everything ground against the stone took on the flavors of the past, so that no bite of food was *sin historia*—without history. As I rolled the stone pin over the hominy, I told myself that I was making my own history with Kerri. Our food would have a bit of our past, present, and hopefully our future in it.

It was hard work, making masa by hand. Hard on my knees, hard on my back. But I liked it. My knees spread to lower my center of gravity. As I ground the hominy, I rocked forward over the metate. The muscles in my shoulders and arms flexed, feeling strain no gym machine could copy. My breasts swung free inside my T-shirt until my nipples were sore from the rubbing. My ass pushed up into the air.

Sweat trickled between my breasts. It must have been seventy outside—typical L.A. December weather—and the kitchen was hotter than that. I pushed a tendril of long black hair from my temple with my hunched shoulder.

Every time I pushed forward on the rolling pin, my shorts pulled tight against my mons. I rocked back and forth, tugging and releasing, teasing my clit with each thrust. Could I come just from that? Every movement sent tingles through me.

I heard the sliding glass door out to our little balcony open. Kerri came back inside the kitchen. "The husks are soaking. Oh, mamácita."

She said that every year when she saw me on my knees on the kitchen floor, and every year, I wasn't sure if I was annoyed or pleased that she thought that I looked sexy like that. How many men in my family had said the same thing to their women? It was like doors to the past opening up and generation after generation repeating the same words in the same scene, our own little lust-filled déjà vu.

"Pity we don't have time," Kerri said. She squatted behind me and stroked me through my shorts. I held still, my hands clutching the rolling pin. She worked her fingers past my panties to pinch my clit. "You have to wait."

I squirmed. Her thumb and finger slipped on my juices and tugged. It felt so good.

"We don't have time," she warned, but her fingers still teased. I moaned.

"Not so tough now, are you, chica?"

Shaking my head, I wriggled back on her fingers.

The downstairs buzzer rang.

"I guess Lisa and Jane are here."

I rocked back on her fingers. "They can wait."

"Don't be such a slut. I'll do you later," she promised as she withdrew her touch. "If I don't have anything better to do, that is."

I threw a ball of masa at her as she ducked out of the kitchen to buzz them into the building.

As our guests climbed the three flights of stairs to our door, I dashed into the bedroom to put on clean clothes. I was tempted to take care of my juicy clit but then they were knocking on the door and Kerri didn't seem to be around to answer it, so I had to rush out of the bedroom before I could do anything about my situation.

Lisa and Jane were veterans of our tamale parties. A lanky punk girl stood in the hallway behind them staring at her ratty shoes.

"This is Tammy. We hope you don't mind us bringing her along," Lisa said.

I smiled and opened the door wider. "Of course not." I caught Tammy's elusive gaze as Lisa swept past me. "Tammy, thanks for coming to help."

She mumbled something as she shuffled after Lisa and plopped down on the couch in the living room.

Jane gave us an apologetic look. "We didn't want to leave her alone. She's been real down. The holidays, you know. They're hard," she whispered.

"Hey, really, she's more than welcome. Room enough for everyone."

Reassured, Jane kissed my cheek. She sniffed the air. "Oh man. It smells like Christmas in here."

The door across the hallway opened.

"Hey! Is it time?" Jimmy asked. "Just let me put on a shirt and we'll be over. We've been smelling that sauce all morning. I'm already starving."

Kerri appeared beside me. I was tempted to give her a piece of my mind for leaving me all tingly and unfulfilled like that, but from the wicked gleam in her eye, I had a feeling she liked me all worked up and frustrated.

As soon as Jimmy and his girlfriend Ann walked in, they grabbed beers from the refrigerator and headed out to the balcony where they set to work unrolling the corn husks. It was funny how people staked out their job and returned to it each year. I could picture my father and uncles sitting out on the patio back home doing the same thing.

After checking that Lisa, Jane, and Tammy were settled in, I went back to the kitchen. Kerri was sneaking bites of pork from the pot again.

"I'm just making sure it's ready. It tastes even better than last year. Did you change your recipe?"

"You know I didn't. And stop acting all innocent." It was hard to look menacing, but I tried.

"About what?"

"You know perfectly well what I'm talking about."

Kerri grinned as she sniffed her fingers. I just about smacked her when Jimmy opened the sliding glass door.

"We have a pile of husks ready to go," he said.

Kerri leaned around the wall that separated the kitchen from the living room. "Lisa! Jane! Showtime! Get your asses in here. You know the drill." She winked at me.

I gave her a dark look and flounced off to set up TV trays for everyone to work on since we couldn't all fit around our tiny kitchen table.

Lisa and Jane made each tamale from start to finish. Kerri, Jimmy, and Ann believed in a production line. One smeared masa over the corn husk, the next one scooped a bit of pork filling inside, and the last one neatly tied the bundle. Tammy spread the masa too thin, tried to put in too much filling, or couldn't tie off the husks right. Every one she made was a mess, and she knew it. She handed them to me, her eyes averted.

I wouldn't lie and say hers were perfect, but I promised her, "They'll taste wonderful. You'll see."

I carried the pile of tamales into the kitchen. As I stood them on end in the steamer, Kerri slipped into the kitchen. She nodded toward our bedroom.

"What?" I asked as I followed her into our bedroom.

She closed the door quietly and wriggled her eyebrows.

"Now? We have guests." I tried to open the door, but she held it closed.

"They'll be busy with the tamales for a while."

"Not that long." I tried to open the door, but she still held it closed.

She nuzzled against my neck. "You're into traditions. How about some traditional make-up sex?"

"We aren't fighting."

"You were fighting pretty hard to keep my fingers inside you earlier."

She unzipped my pants and slid her hand inside them. "Your panties are soaked." Her fingers worked over my swollen clit through the cotton. "Want to take them off?"

Knowing that I shouldn't, I nodded anyway. I wanted those fingers back inside me. "Okay, but quietly."

She tried to kiss me, but I pushed her back until she fell onto our bed. I kicked off my shoes and tugged off my pants while she lazed back and smiled at me. I crawled over her.

"You're a bad influence," I told her.

"You're the one attacking me."

"You better finish what you started, Papi. I swear, if you get me all worked up and walk away from me again, there's going to be a terrible tragedy on the news tonight."

She rolled me over. For a moment, she smirked down at me. Then her expression softened. "Poor baby. So hot and horny. You need it, don't you?"

I made sad eyes and nodded.

Her hand slipped between our bodies. She cupped my mons, barely curving her fingers enough so that I could feel them. I squirmed as I tried to spread my legs. She worked her fingers into my panties.

"Do you want me to take these off you?"

"God, yes."

There was nothing like a lover you knew when you were in a hurry. Confident touches in all the right places; curves that fit together like memory; fingertips that glided over heated skin; shared gasps between soul kisses.

She worked her knee between my legs and bumped against me. It wasn't enough. We tangled legs. I ground hard against her, wet clit to damp mound.

Kerri tasted of red sauce. Her lips moved from my neck down my stomach. She lingered over the soft swell of my belly. I lifted my hips against her. Her fingers traced long swirls on the insides of my thighs.

Our scents mingled and filled the room. Heat flushed my mouth, warmed my hands. She put her mouth over my clit and flicked her tongue.

"I like this tradition," I whispered.

"Shh, Mami. The kids will hear us."

I chuckled. "We're not making that much noise. Oh!"

Her fingers slid in and out of me as she pressed her thumb against my clit. Soon, my thighs were drenched. I grasped her hair.

"You taste so sweet."

She sucked my clit hard, the way I liked it. Back arched, I lifted my hips to her mouth. My body went taut as the finger-fucking and sucking sent me over the edge.

Afterward, we spooned on the bed.

"We should get back before they notice we're gone," she murmured as she flicked my earlobe with her tongue.

"Hmmm," I agreed, but I didn't want to be the first to move.

She pressed her lips to my shoulder. "Come on."

I rolled on my back. The sheets were a tangled mess under us. "I'm too relaxed." But that wasn't true. Energy sizzled through me.

"Come on," she said again, giving my butt a light smack.

We exchanged guilty grins as we dressed. Kerri checked herself in the mirror and fixed the curl that tumbled artfully from her gelled hair. I hoped a touch of cologne would cover the scent of sex on my skin.

I had no idea how long we were gone. No one seemed to notice when we came back in the room, though. I collected the tamales they'd made and put them into the steamer.

After the tamales steamed, everyone took plates, and for one perfect moment, there was contented silence through the apartment. Even Tammy smiled a little. Corn husks piled beside plates. Beers were raised in toasts. Everyone agreed the food was better than the year before. They said that every year.

Jane gathered dirty plates and carried them to the kitchen. Jimmy groaned and complained he ate too much. Ann and Tammy huddled together to gaze at the screen of one of their phones.

For the first time all day, I sank onto the couch with a groan. The cushion was comfortable and worn in the right spots. Kerri handed me a glass of wine. She sat on the arm of the couch and leaned close to me. Her arm went across the back of the cushions and I rested my head against her thigh.

Christmas and tamales—both came wrapped in little packages, and both were filled with love.

VALENTINE

River Light

I knelt as I had been told, stunned. My ears hummed and my skin seemed to vibrate with shock or electricity—I couldn't tell which. My cheeks burned as I realized that I was slick with my own juice as my clit throbbed against the harness I wore.

I kept still, head down and hands clasped behind my back, and waited, mind racing. This was not at all what I had expected. I wanted to cry, to plead with her, but was too proud and was afraid she would slip her hands into my pants and feel how wet I had suddenly become. In fact, I couldn't remember the last time I had been this wet.

Since we had started living together it had become hard for me to get ready for our dates. It was difficult to push the details of our day-to-day living out of my mind. When we had lived separately, the routine of dressing and preparing myself, along with the expectation and nervousness of seeing her, had slipped me into a state of submissive expectation. This nervous unrest brought me to my knees when I finally walked across her threshold.

When Silvia had undressed, each layer was a surprise, and the smell of her skin and her sweat seemed new again each time. Now I knew intimately the contents of her closet, her hair products, her favorite stockings. There were so few surprises left, it seemed.

It was Valentine's Day, the first since we had begun sharing a home, and I put on my harness, hoping she would not walk in before I got past the awkward stage—getting the right strap through the correct loop and into the appropriate buckle. When I finished dressing, I stood and inspected myself in the mirror. I looked good. My black jeans and pressed shirt were casual enough so as not to look out of place at a party, but dressy enough for a formal dinner. The bulge in my pants looked inviting but not vulgar. My nails were neatly manicured, and my dark hair newly cut by my barber. She had not told me her plans, but I was ready for anything, or so I thought.

Dinner was exquisite. She had found a lovely restaurant that we had never been to, and we ate well. She looked beautiful. The dress she wore was the same one she had worn on our first date, and it always made me feel like an awkward teenage boy next to her. We talked and reminisced, and laughed at the waiter's obvious envy at my basket and curiosity at the collar I wore.

As dinner progressed, I felt a slow rising of apprehension as I became more cognizant of her energy. She had a calm assurance, and a level attentiveness, which set off warning bells. Living together did not mean that I had lost all of my fear of her. I caught her watching me pensively at times, and knew the look to mean that she was assessing how much I could take. My palms were clammy, and I kept taking deep breaths to calm myself. She had not said that we would be playing tonight, but by dinner's end I knew we would be.

When we got to the car, she took the keys. I sat in the passenger seat, feeling awkward without the wheel in front of me.

I tried to keep myself calm as we drove through the city streets. We turned into a tree-lined side street, and suddenly I knew where we were going. Casey's place. Casey was Silvia's top and one mean son of a bitch. I had never played with her, nor had I ever watched her and Silvia play, but I knew her by reputation and from watching a few public scenes. She and Silvia saw each other once a month, and had done so for many years. Coming here was definitely an unexpected turn of events.

As we got out of the car, Silvia clipped the leash to my collar. I dropped to the appropriate two steps behind her and to the right. It felt reassuring to fall into the protocol that defined the core of our relationship.

When we stepped through the doorway my eyes instantly riveted on Casey. She was standing in the center of the living room dressed from head to toe in supple black leather: cap, bound chest covered in a white sleeveless T-shirt and motorcycle jacket, gauntlets, jean-cut leather pants over a bulge I could see from across the room, and her heavy motorcycle boots. Even I could appreciate how incredibly hot she looked. She epitomized female masculinity. Next to her I felt like a soft butch.

"Take your clothes off." Silvia's voice precluded argument. Hands shaking, I stripped down to my boxers, and then catching her uncompromising look, shucked those off too.

"He's yours till midnight," she said, and then to me, "kneel."

I knelt as I had been told, stunned.

This was my present? Being given away on Valentine's Day? My mind raced. I knew I had made comments about jerking off to the thought of being topped by another butch, but had I actually said I would want it in real life? Did it even matter, considering how wet I was?

It did matter, damn it, because this was the last thing in the world that I had expected, and wet or not, I did not know if I really wanted it. I wanted to be snuggling at home with my love, whispering sweet nothings or licking her boots.

Maybe this was not *my* Valentine's gift at all; maybe this was Casey's. My heart sank. On the other hand, I suspected that watching something like this was the kind of thing that would get Silvia off, so maybe this was actually Casey's gift to her. That made me feel better. I was relatively certain that my Mistress could not watch someone else hurt me to any great extent without her protective instincts taking over.

Casey sauntered up and Silvia passed the leash over to her and stepped back. Casey tugged on the leash and I crawled to her feet, feeling foolish and very naked with my limp packing dick hanging out. The leather that stretched tight across *her* dick outlined the bulge of a very large, very firm cock down her left leg. When I got to her she yanked me to kneeling and stepped up to me, the taut leash pressing my face hard into her crotch. The smell and feel of leather was intoxicating, and I caught myself drooling at the thought of the soft leather and firm bulge under my tongue.

"Has it ever had a fist in its ass?" My heart stopped.

"No, but go ahead."

"Any restrictions?" Casey asked.

Silvia shrugged. "No permanent marks."

Behind me I could hear my Top let herself out and lock the door behind her. Just like that. So it wasn't her Valentine's gift after all—I felt sick.

Using the leash, Casey yanked my chin up. Only then did

she look down at me, the barest hint of a smile curling her lips.

"Tonight, you are going to beg me to fuck you." Her voice had that maddening self-assurance of a Top who hadn't bottomed in much too long.

Fuck you, I don't beg, I thought, but kept my mouth shut.

I didn't see her hand coming, but it caught me hard across the cheek. I tried to yank away, and she hit me a second time.

"Hold the fuck still!" She hit me again. "Silvia says you are a good boi, but if I see that look on your face again, I'm going to tell her just how wrong she is."

"But I am a good boi!" I blurted out, fighting back tears. This was so unfair.

"Are you?" she sneered, "I suspect that Silvia's judgment has been impaired when it comes to you, but I guess we'll see."

She tugged on the leash and led me to the center of the room. Kicking a throw rug to the side, she revealed a recessed ring. She deftly clipped the collar to the ring, forcing my head to the floor. This left my ass sticking up in the air and my weight supported by either my forehead or my arms. Not a position I wished to be in. I began to lower my belly to the floor.

"Keep that ass up and spread your legs!" she snapped. I did as I was told, feeling my face flush with shame at my vulnerability. She walked around behind me and I felt a gloved hand slide up my thigh and grasp my cock. She began to jerk me off, stroking along my shaft and pulling back firmly. My clit began to throb at the rhythmic contact and at the picture of a leather-clad Daddy teasing his naked boi. I bit back a groan. I was going to make Silvia proud, I was not going to give Casey any reason to call my Top a liar—but that didn't mean I was going to like it. My legs started to shake. *Fuck you*, I thought, *fuck you, fuck you, fuck you.*

"You like that, boi? You like a Daddy's strong hand?"

When I didn't reply, her hand came down hard on my ass, and I jumped. Then I was getting a spanking like I never had before. There was no warm-up and each blow jerked my body forward, pulling hard on my collar. I cried out with each strike and it took everything I had to remain still for the stinging pain. I was frantic for it to stop, but it just went on and on. My ass was burning hot, and to my horror tears seeped from the corners of my eyes. Finally it got through to me that she was not going to stop until I answered her question. I felt sick at the thought of admitting that Casey's cavalier hand job had been turning me on, but I needed the spanking to stop.

"Yes," I said, my voice almost a whisper. She stopped.

"Excuse me?"

"Yes," I repeated.

"Yes *what*?" This time it was her belt that cut across my cheeks, and I screamed.

"Yes, I like a Daddy's strong hand!"

Then she was spanking me again, but this time almost gently and in much more private spots. It felt good, too good. Just when I thought I was going to give myself away, she stopped and pulled my cheeks apart to reveal my asshole. I wanted to crawl into a hole.

"And do you like it in the ass, boi?"

"Yes, I like it in the ass," I replied hastily. But the belt cracked across my cheeks anyway, and this time I did try to get away, flattening myself to the floor, only to scramble back to position in a panic. The second blow didn't come, and I felt a wave of gratitude.

"Sir," she said.

"Yes, I like it in the ass, Sir," I said through my stifled sobs.

I heard the snap of a glove and felt her lube-covered fingers probing my asshole.

Oh god, she's going to try to fist me, I thought as her fingers pressed deeper and her knuckles dug into my cheeks. However, it was a large butt plug that I felt next, and my ass swallowed it up with embarrassing ease. It felt so good to have my ass filled. Maybe she'd let me suck her cock too. I could do that, I thought, I could suck her cock. That was a boi thing to do, suck a Daddy's cock. Suddenly I was jarred back to the moment as Casey unbuckled my harness and slipped off my dick. She rubbed my cunt with her foot, and I gasped. The toe of her boot alternately rubbed my clit and tried to force its way into me.

I'm a boi! I wanted to blurt out as she walked around me. Her boot was under my face, soaked in my juice.

"Lick it clean." I hastily did as I was told.

"You sure are enjoying yourself," she sneered. "You're dripping on my clean floor. You have your ass up in the air like some bitch in heat, waiting to be mounted. You're slobbering over your own cunt juice." Half of me hated her, and the other half just wanted her to touch me again. When her boot was clean she moved away.

"You like this?" she asked, pushing the plug deeper into me.

"Yes, Sir. I like it, Sir," I gasped.

"And this? Do you like this too?" Her gloved finger reached down and began stroking my clit at the same time as she fucked my ass, sending shock waves through me.

"Yes, Sir. I like that too, Sir," I groaned. My whole body was on fire; every inch of me trembled with desire. She continued, firm, smooth and slow. My cunt began to ache and burn with emptiness. I could feel my wetness soaking my thighs and I desperately wanted something in my mouth. I felt like I was going out of my mind. I could feel my orgasm building, fire moving from my core outward, filling me with electricity and heat.

Suddenly her hands were gone and the butt plug pulled out. I cried out in disappointment and strained my ass toward her. There was a long silence. I could tell she was behind me, not moving, just watching me. Then, "I think I should just leave you like this." She began to walk away.

"No!"

Her footsteps stopped.

"No? You don't want me to stop?"

"No, please, Sir, I don't." I needed her to come back, I'd go crazy if she left me like this.

"Do you want me to fuck you?"

"Yes, Sir, I want you to fuck me, Sir," I blurted before I even thought about it.

"Beg." It was not a command. It was simply a statement, said with no intonation at all. I wanted to scream. My body was shaking with desire and rage. Tears streamed down my cheeks. I could hardly beg for my own Mistress, let alone for this obnoxious, self-centered, conceited show-off with a bad case of Top's disease. She had no fucking idea what this was like.

"Please," I whispered. I couldn't do it. I was not going to let her have the satisfaction of seeing me grovel. "Please fuck me, Sir." I hated her. "Oh god, please fuck me." The wood that I rested my forehead on was damp from my tears and snot. "Please, please, please fuck me, Sir, please." To my disgust, I was babbling. "Please fuck me, oh please just fuck me."

"Do you need my cock in your cunt, bitch?"

"Yes, Sir, I need your cock in my cunt, Sir. Please, Sir..."

She unclipped the leash, and I straightened up painfully. Mesmerized by her hands, I watched her undo her fly and pull out her cock. She turned and walked into the bedroom, with me crawling after her, leash dragging on the ground.

"On your back on the bed, legs spread wide." I did as I

was told, spreading my legs as wide as I could and turning my burning face away from her. I couldn't believe that I had just obediently lain on my back for a butch. As she moved on top of me, she grabbed my jaw and turned my head so I was looking into her eyes. Then her cock brushed my cunt and I arched, trying to reach for her.

"That's right, reach for it." And I did, struggling for contact, knowing she could see all my desire in my eyes. She slipped her gloved fingers into my mouth and I sucked on them greedily. By the time she moved into me, in one smooth thrust, my head was spinning and my eyes were blurry. And she was good. Fuck, she was good. I could feel my orgasm building in all corners of my body, and when I was about to come, there was nothing in the world but her cock and my cunt.

"Oh god, can I come? Please, can I come? Oh god, oh god, please let me come!" I was frantic. "Oh please, I can't help it, I can't stop it! Please, Sir, may I come?"

"Did Silvia say you could?" Her voice was amused and she did not slow down in the least. I panicked. She hadn't. I fought, trying to get out from under Casey, trying to get away from her cock. She grabbed my arms and pressed them painfully into the bed above my head, her full weight on my wrists and in my cunt. My Mistress had not given me permission, and I was about to lose it and shame myself and her, and I couldn't stop myself.

"Boi, you may come." Silvia's voice came from somewhere behind me, and I did, my body exploding again and again, my voice ripped raw from screaming.

As I became aware of my surroundings again, I felt Silvia pressed against one side of me and Casey on the other. She must have circled around and come back in the back door.

Happy Valentine's Day to us, I thought.

BIRTHDAY
BUTCH

Teresa Noelle Roberts

'd love to say JT and I met at a seedy bar, like characters in a '50s pulp novel with a cheesy title along the lines of *Women in the Shadows* or *Cruel Female Lusts*. Actually a mutual friend introduced us, and I don't think Edgar imagined that we'd hook up. He just knew that JT was looking for someone who'd tend bar at her birthday party and I do a bit of bartending. People seem to enjoy having a tiny slip of a woman in a deliciously slinky vintage cocktail dress and high, high heels mixing them drinks. Eye candy for those who like pretty ladies, retro fun for everyone, and I make a mean Cosmo and pour a perfect Guinness, if I do say so myself.

As soon as I met JT, something pinged my radar—not my gaydar, because Edgar had already mentioned we were both dykes as he introduced us, but the other radar, the one that found women who might particularly fancy a woman like me, a woman who looked like she was all sweet curves, but knew how to bring a submissive type to her knees. JT was big and buff and loud—and absolutely gorgeous—but I sensed something else in her, something that wanted to stop, if only for a little while, being so damn tough. And I think she sensed the steel inside my fragile trappings, even if she wasn't sure, initially, what to make of the combination.

Even before I did the smoldering, yet arrogant sideways glance, even before I crossed my legs in a way that showed off my Cuban-heeled stockings, hellishly high heels, and kitten-with-a-whip tattoo on my calf, JT looked me up and down stealthily, yet wouldn't meet my eyes. She held my hand a little too long when she shook it, yet stood farther away than I'd expect a big, good-looking butch to do with a pretty femme. Especially not when I'd made a point of mentioning I wasn't dating anyone as soon as I saw JT's big brown eyes, strong arms, and mischievous smile.

A smile that seemed less confident around me than it did around other people.

Some women might have found that discouraging.

I found it promising.

There's cool distance, the kind you maintain as a barrier between you and someone you don't particularly like.

And then there's hot distance, which is what happens when you like someone a lot, but are baffled by what you're feeling and aren't ready to act on it.

This was hot distance.

And I intended to close it.

I watched JT with other women as I served drinks at her birthday party. She flirted. She danced close, even with women who were definitely part of a couple. Hell, she danced close with guys, including Edgar, who was there with his husband. She hugged and smooched and grabbed butts. She laughed a lot, deep and sexy and hearty, the way I like to see a woman laugh.

Especially when she's big and strong, with hands that could span my waist (at least if I'm wearing a corset).

But not with me. With me, it was all shy glances from downcast eyes and the kind of "pleases" and "thank yous" and gentle good behavior that would make a churchgoing grandma proud.

It made me giddy as if I'd been drinking just enough champagne for the bubbles to get to me.

Maybe she wasn't sure how to treat someone who was essentially the hired help for the night, but could just as easily have been a party guest. But I didn't think so. I ventured a guess that she'd read something in my body language, my carriage, the way I walked in my heels as strong and confident as she did in her Docs, and it touched some part of her that wanted a small, soft woman who could make her feel small and soft herself. She wasn't quite sure how to go about courting a domme in a pretty vintage dress, though, especially when we hadn't met at a munch for kinksters or a play party, and it made her adorably shy.

Certainly she made a lot of excuses to fetch drinks for her friends and visit the bar again to half talk to me, to not quite meet my eyes. And I took advantage of every one of those visits to brush my hand against hers, to lean forward so she could look at my cleavage (and then look away again, a telltale red on her cheeks), to lead her shamelessly into flirtation despite her best efforts to remain polite and respectful.

JT was definitely intrigued, but I thought it might take more than one night to get her to take the bait. After all, we'd just met, and through Edgar, who was lovingly dubbed Cottage Cheese Boy because he was milder than vanilla.

Then a couple of drunk, rowdy bois decided to do my work for me. After the cake was cut, but before the presents were opened, the cry went up, led by one particular couple, "Time for JT's birthday spanking!"

With that, I stopped washing glasses and leaned on the bar to watch the show.

JT started out protesting and squirming and doing all the things you're supposed to do when overenthusiastic, tipsy friends decide to smack your ass in public.

In the midst of her struggles JT glanced over at me.

Very slowly, very deliberately, I winked and nodded.

Her eyes widened. Her struggles continued, but less emphatically and, at least to my eyes, less believably.

Since everyone else was watching JT and her friends roughhousing, I leaned forward and cupped my breasts so they spilled out of the neckline of the strapless dress I wore. A quick flash of nipple and they were back in my dress, but I think I made the point: Get spanked and you might get these.

JT licked her lips and relaxed visibly.

The slighter of the bois grabbed her wrists and pushed her forward, pinning her wrists down to the table so her butt stuck out. Seconds later, the other laid a good whack on her ass.

JT's body stiffened and she yelped.

On the second whack, though, she sagged, yielding.

I clenched. That moment when a strong woman surrenders, even if someone else provoked it, is always delicious to see.

She turned toward me again, her eyes wide and stricken, her mouth slightly open. I could tell she was breathing heavily.

For the entire time she was being spanked—first fairly seriously by the bois who'd instigated it, then a playful smack or two from most of the guests—she kept her face turned toward me, letting me watch each expression that passed over her face. Playful amusement changed to panic, and panic changed to a delicious mixture of panic and arousal. The arousal grew as her friends continued to torment her, and the panic eased back to nervousness or self-consciousness, but never fled altogether.

Caught in the heat myself, I squirmed and rubbed my slick lips against my lace panties. I wanted so much to order everyone else away, strip off JT's jeans, and continue spanking her properly, catching the sweet spot where thighs curved up into ass, lingering after each stroke to let the pain morph to pleasure, then pinching the reddened, tender flesh to morph pleasure back to pain. Wanted to fuck her senseless once she'd been thoroughly spanked, or perch on the table, thighs open, fist my hands in her hair and force her— not because she'd need to be forced but because it would be fun for both of us to pretend—to lick me to orgasm.

The gathering grew more and more raucous as the guests cheered and laughed and counted loudly, even though the count had long since exceeded JT's possible age.

Some of the other guests must have noticed how she trembled and gasped, how her hands clenched and unclenched on the table, how she cocked her ass toward the spanking hands.

But she was still turned toward me, so only I got to watch as her face flushed and her eyes widened. Got to see the astonished need blossom on her handsome face.

Got to see her mouth at me, "Please."

I nodded almost curtly, though I melted on the inside from a combination of lust and tenderness. I doubt anyone noticed, enthralled as they were with the spectacle. But JT did.

Her eyes closed, then opened again in astonishment. She screamed in perfect silence as the orgasm unleashed itself. Her gaze locked into mine and I shared an echo of every tremor she felt.

Even though it was presumptuous, given that nothing had happened other than some significant eye contact at the right moment, I yielded to the impulse to mouth, "Mine."

This time she couldn't hide the gasp or the convulsion.

Most of her friends began to chuckle knowingly, except for

the ones who were too busy kissing and groping their dates, turned on by the unexpected show.

I'm 99 percent sure the instigators would have been happy to have their wickedly fun way with her, either later or right there and then in the middle of the party. And under other circumstances, JT might have let them—they were a good-looking pair, both lean and leggy with small, perky breasts and short, sexily messy hair. Instead, she laughed and let the couple engulf her in a hug. Then she smacked both their asses with all the strength in her body. JT's not a small girl, not by any means, so they both yelped and jumped back. "Let's see," JT said loudly, in a voice that sounded only slightly shaky and maybe only because I was listening for that telltale post-orgasmic quiver, "Mackenzie's birthday's in June and Laura's is in October. Lots of time to plot and scheme. Wait for it, guys. Just wait for it."

A number of the guests chimed in, offering to help with the plot—evidently Mackenzie and Laura instigated all kinds of amusing trouble for their friends and payback was going to be a very entertaining bitch. It's possible the tables could have turned right then, if JT hadn't proclaimed loudly, "After that, I need a drink," shaken off her friends, and headed to the bar.

She moved with a sexy butch swagger, but her face was soft and eager as she approached me. She ordered a dirty martini, obviously so I could take a little time fussing over it. "Dirty martini for a dirty girl," I whispered as I pretended to look for the jar of olives that was in plain sight on a shelf under the bar. "You came, didn't you?"

She nodded, her face once again flushed. "Twice. But only because I was looking at you. Playing rough makes me wet, but it's never enough to get me off. Not until you told me to come tonight." Her voice, already soft, dropped even lower, to a quiet burr that vibrated my clit.

"Do you have plans for after the party?" Before she could answer, before she could even open her mouth again, I said, "Change them. I can give you a birthday treat you'll really like. But only if you're good."

She nodded, her face gone vacant with desire.

"One dirty martini for the birthday girl," I said teasingly loudly, handing her the drink and shooing her away with a wink and a mouthed "later."

I don't know if she'd planned to hook up with one of the other guests. But she managed to encourage everyone out the door just after midnight, although a not very surprising number of the guests had drifted off in twos and threes right after the spanking incident, in search of privacy or maybe opportunities for their own bit of exhibitionism.

JT was at the bar as soon as the last women were out the door. "You'll still have to pay me until two o'clock," I said as dryly and calmly as I could.

"You're worth it." She chuckled throatily.

She stopped chuckling when I stalked around the bar and sidled up close to her.

Even with my four-inch heels, she was a few inches taller than I am—so I grabbed the back of her hair and pulled her down to me.

"First order," I breathed. "Kiss me. Kiss me like you mean it. You may hug me, but no touching me otherwise yet. Right now, I'm interested in a good kiss."

Those strong, muscled arms were around me before I finished talking, and her lips closed on mine.

I didn't taste gin and olives—I don't think she ever drank that dirty martini. I tasted a little butter-and-sugar goodness from the birthday cake frosting that lingered at the corners of her mouth.

Then I tasted only her, and that was headier than any drink I'd ever mixed.

JT held me close, almost lifting me off the floor. It was more forceful than I'd normally want a sub to be until we knew each other well, but forceful or not, she was trembling with need and nerves, and being so close to her let me enjoy that. She kissed me like she meant it, all right, but stayed one nanosecond behind me, letting me set the pace Her body was fire-hot and her hands shook and I could tell she wanted to grind against my thigh, caress the bounty of my breasts, raise my satin skirt to check out my garter belt and tiny (and very wet) lace panties.

She didn't, though.

Nor did she hesitate when I pulled away and told her to strip. In fact, her clothes came off so fast I'm surprised she didn't break her boot laces or rip the buttons off her shirt.

She wasn't wearing a bra.

Her body was so beautiful I had to look away and bark, "Fold your clothes and put them on the chair. I can't abide slobs," so I didn't abandon all my lovely kinky notions and just start exploring every inch of that strong but curvy lusciousness. (I hoped to do that at some point, because I'd enjoy it thoroughly—I'm a greedy little domme and I like to play with my girls in every possible way. Just not yet.)

Her eyes widened, but she obeyed without saying anything but "Yes…Ma'am." She hesitated then, "Should I call you Ma'am? Mistress?"

I smiled then, a very predatory smile that should have showed fangs. "Tina will do—but I like the way you think. Now turn for me. Let me look at you."

"Yes, Tina." It was obvious from the awkwardly self-conscious way she moved that JT had escaped the teen modeling classes I'd saved my pennies to take. She didn't know what to do with her hands and stumbled over her own feet turning around. But she was grinning like she was high, and moisture glistened on her strong thighs, and her ass, formerly concealed by comfortably loose jeans, was round and perfect enough to make Jennifer Lopez green with envy—round and perfect and still slightly pink from the earlier spanking.

I stalked over, dug my short but elegantly red nails into that perfect curve. She flinched, then sighed with pleasure. I nudged her thighs apart, stroked at her wet sex until her hips began to work of their own accord and her breath came in little gasps. Then I said, "No. Not until I tell you. And don't say a word, not unless it's to say 'red' because you want me to stop."

I felt her body stiffen, but she obeyed.

Obeyed as I continued to stroke her slick, swollen clit and insinuate my fingers into her drenched pussy.

Obeyed as I bent her over the couch and spanked her ass just as I'd imagined earlier, until it was so red it was almost glowing. Tears of excitement flowed down her thighs, and tears of frustration hung in her eyes when I pulled her up for a rough kiss, but she still obeyed. Obeyed when I grabbed her abandoned belt and snapped it against that beautiful, reddened ass.

At that, she flinched away, then arched back, seeking more. She sucked her breath in on a hiss and let it out with a moan, but she didn't speak.

And even though her pussy was as wet as any I'd seen in my life, and twitched visibly with each smack of the belt, she didn't come.

Not until I grabbed one end of the belt in each hand and laid it across her throat, applying no pressure, but letting her know I could if I chose. "Come," I ordered. "Come now."

And she did, with a cry that shook a smaller orgasm loose in me.

Suddenly unsteady in my heels, I dropped the belt and plopped down onto the couch, encouraging JT to follow. I ended up with her lying across my lap, her face zoned out and tear-streaked and blissful.

It took a while before either of us said anything. Finally she spoke in a small, soft, floaty voice. "What may I do for you, Tina?"

"The mind boggles. I can think of all sorts of delicious things. But right now, just lie here with me and catch your breath."

Then I grabbed her nipple and gave it a twisting pinch. "Oh yeah...and you could come again. Now."

And she did, arching her back and scrambling against the couch as pleasure claimed her. "What...the...hell," she gasped out. "I've never come from something like that."

"Never had someone tell you to, either, I bet."

When she shook her head, I laughed and said, "Oh, JT, we are going to have so much fun."

And then I kissed her, letting her taste the remnants of my lipstick, letting her feel me claiming her the way a butch like her needed to be claimed.

BORN TO RIDE

Beth Wylde

I know what I like and I'm not ashamed to go after it. Tonight I've got a specific target in mind. Like a lioness in the jungle, I'm on the prowl, and only one thing will sate my appetite. A butch, but not just any butch. No soft girls. No femmes playing dress-up. No college bois or preppy *GQ* wannabes. I want a hard, aggressive, dominant woman. Tall and bulky with big muscles and close-cropped hair. Maybe even a tat or two, because ink done right on a macho chick is sooo sexy. She'll be wearing leather or well-worn denim and a tight T-shirt or tank with no bra.

She'll have a nice fat cock packed tight in her pants. One that she actually knows how to use. She'll treat me like royalty in public. Call me baby or sweetheart and wait on my every need, then force me to my knees to suck her dick behind closed doors. The type of masculine female who knows how to please a woman and make her beg for mercy all at the same time.

Just the thought of her has my panties damp and my breasts

tingling. My clit is throbbing and my large nipples are visible even through my bra. I'm so turned on I could explode. It's all I can do not to reach down between my legs and bring myself off. I manage to restrain myself, knowing that job belongs to someone else tonight. First, I have to set the perfect trap.

The dress I've picked out is red. Deep, dark red. Scarlet really, with peep-toe slingback high heels and lipstick to match. The design is daringly low cut and tight, barely restraining my bountiful breasts and hugging my ample curves. The perfect outfit to lure my prey.

My plain brown hair has new auburn highlights and is put together in an intricate updo, held together with a few pins and a pretty clip. The hairstyle serves several purposes tonight. Having it off my neck keeps me cool and gives my handsome butch easy access for nibbles and kisses and hopefully a bite or two. If she wants to get rougher later she'll have plenty of hair to run her fingers through and grab onto. I love to have my hair tugged while I'm getting fucked from behind.

I spin in the mirror and admire the way the dress flares, flashing tempting glimpses of my thighs and my tiny boy-cut panties.

I grab my purse and keys as I head out the door. My destination is clear: Anna and Eve. It's all lesbian, all the time. The lounge is an eclectic mix of dykes. Butches, bois, femmes, and everything in between. A veritable lesbian smorgasbord, and I can't wait to sample the fare.

The parking lot is packed when I pull in. A good sign. There are several trucks and a few sports cars, even a motorcycle or two, though they all seem to be rice burners. No self-respecting hard-core butch would be caught dead on one of those. As I park, I spot one real bike. The lone Harley Fat Boy parked off to the side could definitely prove promising. The shiny black-

and-chrome monster looks well loved, and I can just picture the commanding type of woman it would take to handle a bike like that. The image in my mind sends another jolt of lust through me that has my vulva begging for attention. I need to get inside and find my woman fast.

I hand the girl at the door a five and ignore her frank appraisal. She doesn't even look old enough to drink, so having her card me is a bit degrading. I suffer through it in hopes that I'll find what I'm craving just beyond the double doors. No such luck.

The minute I enter, I'm ready to leave. My hopes for the evening are crushed. The room is full of femmes as far as the eye can see. An ocean of girly-girls. There isn't a single woman in the room that even comes close to my fantasy.

Did my invitation to the high femme conference get lost in the mail? Did someone revoke my femme card altogether? What the hell is going on?

I don't see one pair of leather pants or faded jeans in the room. Where are all the burly butches? Where is my motorcycle-riding goddess? Dear god. I've died and gone to lipstick lesbian hell.

The women all turn in my direction, looking as dejected to see me as I am to see them. A few smile and turn their attention back to their fruity drinks, but I don't grin back. I'm past sympathy at this point. I'm pissed. I know there's a very unwelcoming scowl on my face and I don't care. I'm not even sure who is angrier over the situation, me or my cunt. I spent quite a pretty penny on my outfit for the evening and lots of time on my makeup and hair. Now all that effort is wasted. The few soft butches and bois I manage to spot are glued firmly to their girlfriend's sides, so even if I was feeling up to their company they wouldn't be available.

I know I should leave. It's early enough that I can make it

to another club if I hurry. There are a few other places in town that cater to our community, but Anna and Eve is the only all-female establishment in the city. I like the laid-back atmosphere at A&E, and if I go home I'll just end up eating a half gallon of Chunky Monkey to console my lonely libido. I might as well have a drink. It will be easier on my hips than the ice cream.

I order a white wine spritzer and catch up on Mona, the bartender's, love life. Before I know it my glass is empty and she's poured me another. I'm babbling on about what I want in a woman and she listens patiently the way all good friends and bartenders do. She starts to fix me a third when I stop her. I decline politely and toss a twenty on the bar.

Mona shoves it back at me. "It's on the house tonight. You look like you need it. Maybe you'd like something stronger? Want me to fix you a shot? I've got some fine scotch in the store-room. I've been waiting for a good excuse to pop it open."

I think about her offer for all of a minute. "Sure. What the hell? I've only got the twenty on me, though. I was hoping to find someone willing to pick up the tab, and me."

She arches a finely waxed eyebrow. "I kinda figured that. I wish you would have called me earlier. I could have saved you a trip."

"You knew it was going to be ladies' night?"

Mona laughs. "I had a clue. They hosted a bachelorette party in here this afternoon. Linda thought it would be funny to throw Jenny's party here at the club."

I know the confusion is clear on my face. "Why here? Jenny is straight as a stick."

Mona nods. "Yeah, supposedly. Linda thought it might knock some sense into her. She's had a crush on that girl for years. Linda's hoping she'll come over to the dark side." The last is said with a chuckle. It's a running joke between us.

I can't help my curiosity. Jenny certainly wouldn't be Linda's first convert. "Did it work?"

Mona snickered. "Let's just say that Jenny won't be walking down the isle with Mark in the morning. She probably won't be able to walk anywhere at all, the way the two of them were carrying on when they left."

I lay my head on the counter next to my empty glass and moan. "Ugh. That is just too depressing."

"What is?"

I sit back up. "Even the straight girls are getting more pussy than me."

Mona smiles sincerely and replaces my spritzer glass with a shot glass. "Just another good reason to get blind drunk. I'll rush into the back and bring out the scotch."

As she turns to go, several women step up to the bar and order drinks, preventing her from leaving. Her eyebrows arch again in perfect synchronization and I know she's thought of something.

She motions me behind the bar and whispers in my ear, "The scotch is in the back. Just go straight down the hall, first door on your left. You'll see it on the desk. Bring it back here. I might even have one with you."

It seems silly to be so impatient. I know I should just wait for Mona to finish up with her current customers and then go get the liquor herself. I'm feeling antsy, though, and I figure the distraction will be good for me.

The hall is dark and it takes a moment for my eyes to adjust. The door is right where Mona said it would be, but it's closed. I open it. The desk she mentioned is easy to spot, since it takes over almost half the room, but there is no bottle of liquor on it. Instead, a big, black pair of shitkickers fills my vision. The sight is a bit shocking. My eyes start at the soles of the boots and work their way up until they zoom in directly on the owner of the footwear. Just my luck. I go looking for a manly woman and find myself a man instead. His cowboy hat is tipped down low over his face and he's propped so haphazardly in his chair it's tempting to wait and watch him bust his ass. My temper makes a quick return at his presence in the all-female sanctuary of the club.

"What the hell are you doing lurking in here? This is a women's-only club."

My mystery man laughs and I squint harder to see. The sound is higher then it should be and for the first time I realize that the shoes propped up on the desk are rather small for a guy. *Oh god!* "Um. Shit. Uh, I'll just go back out front and get busy pulling my feet out of my mouth. Sorry to have bothered you."

She puts her feet on the floor and leans forward, stopping me with her husky request. "Hold on now, sugar. What's your rush? You didn't come back here just to yell at me and run away, did you?"

I have to think hard to explain. Her deep Southern accent has me mesmerized. "Mona sent me to get her a special bottle of scotch. She said it would be on the desk in the storeroom. I'll just go let her know I couldn't find it."

Her laugh is warm and deep and starts me tingling all over again. It takes me a minute to realize she's speaking to me. Most of my brain is too busy focusing on my clit and what this fine butch in front of me could do to it.

"This isn't the storeroom, honey. That's the second door on the right. This is my office. I'm Shane, the owner of Anna and Eve."

She stands up and moves toward me. I swallow a moan and mentally send Mona my thanks. Whether she sent me to the wrong room on purpose or not doesn't matter.

Shane is very close to six feet tall and muscled all over. The faintest edge of a tattoo peeks out from the collar of her T-shirt just below her brush cut. I've never seen a woman more macho, and it's all I can do not to drop to my knees and beg her to fuck me. The outline of what she has stuffed in her Levi's is unmistakable. I know my nipples are hard once more and I don't try to hide it. I want her, bad, and I'll do anything to prove it!

Shane grins and her even, white teeth leave me panting. I'm suddenly reminded of a line in a fairy tale I heard long ago: "All the better to eat you with, my dear." *Oh yes, please do.*

"Looks like Mona gave you the wrong directions."

I shake my head and move in for the kill. "I don't think so. Her directions seem just perfect to me."

"So it's going to be like that?"

I nod, too captivated to form a real reply.

In response Shane moves closer until my eyes are level with her breasts. Her nipples are clearly visible through the tight black tee and as hard as my own. *No bra. Thank you, Lord.*

"Do you like to ride?"

That's a loaded question. It could mean so many things, and my answer to all of them would be yes. I nod again. She probably thinks I'm a little slow, but I don't care. The only thing I'm concerned with at the moment is her dick and how fast I can get her to use it.

Shane walks off to the side of the room and pulls two motorcycle helmets out of a nearby closet. My clit is so swollen I'm not sure I can walk. I do manage to find my voice though. "The Harley is yours, isn't it?"

She gets a dreamy look on her face and I know I'm right. "Yes, it is. You like bikes?"

I make my move, thrusting my breasts out and running my red-lacquered fingernails down one of Shane's bulging biceps. "I like *real* bikes, and the women that ride them."

The gleam in her eyes as she stares into my cleavage tells me I've won. "Come on, then." She hands me one of the helmets. "I'll take you on a ride you won't forget."

Judging by the size of her hands and what she has tucked in her jeans, I bet she will. Mona pops into my head for just a second and I have a brief war with my conscience. "I should let Mona know where I'm going. She might get worried."

Shane seems to understand. "No problem. Hang on. I'll let her know you're with me."

Shane reaches over to the desk phone and pushes the first button on the side to turn on the speaker. I can hear it ringing. Mona picks up, sounding flustered. "What do you need, boss? I'm busy as hell out here and your new trainee didn't bother to show up tonight."

"Just wanted to let ya know that your friend is with me. We're going for a ride."

"Nicole is with you? I wondered where she'd disappeared to."

I couldn't stay silent. "Mona, you told me the first room on the left was the storeroom."

Her chuckle is easily audible, even above all the calls in the background for drinks. "Did I? Oops. My bad. Talk to you tomorrow, hun." She sounds totally unrepentant. "Take good care of her, Shane. Nicole is very special."

Shane is staring straight at me. "Yes, she is. Will do, darlin'. Talk to ya tomorrow."

Shane's strong arm is the only thing holding me up on the way to the parking lot. She's warm and smells so good. A subtle hint of cologne and hard woman. I'm liable to come the minute I sit on her bike.

"Here we are." Shane touches the bike reverently and gets herself settled on the beast. "Hop on."

She holds the bike balanced as I scoot in close behind her. Short dresses and big bikes don't go well together. Hopefully we aren't going out on the highway, or the people we pass by are going to get a free show. I can feel my ass on full display. Oh well. It's a small price to pay.

One of Shane's large hands reaches back and grabs my knee, pulling me in tighter. "Wouldn't want you to fall off, now would we?"

She doesn't have to worry about that. I'm an experienced rider, both on bikes and off. My crotch is so snug against her 501s I know she can feel the heat between my legs. I hope I don't leave a wet spot on her ass.

I shake my head against her back in answer and she turns the key. The black monster roars to life and I know there is going to be a wet spot on the leather when I get off.

Shane's left hand stays on my leg longer than necessary, caressing my skin until I'm shivering. "Are you cold?"

I shake my head in answer again. The goose bumps are pure arousal and Shane is like a living furnace. I doubt anyone could be cold while wrapped around her powerful body.

Thank god for back country roads. I'm normally not so trusting of strangers, but I know Mona wouldn't have let me go if Shane wasn't all right. We pull over after about ten minutes or so of riding. I'm so turned on I'm thrumming. If I don't get some relief soon I'm going to die. Shane turns to face me, pulling off her helmet and then mine. My look of urgent need is reflected in her face and I know we both have the same thing in mind.

She leans forward and I move to meet her. Our lips clash and the resulting kiss is far from gentle. Shane dominates me. Her hands grab my ass and pull me forward. She picks me up like I don't weigh a thing and settles me in her lap. My legs are over hers and I'm squirming to try to get our centers aligned. It's not going to work in our current position, but that doesn't make me stop grinding my pelvis against her stomach.

She takes pity on me and moves one hand from my backside, across my hip and down where I need it the most. She's stroking the very center of my silky panties and I know I'm liable to come from the friction. I pull back with heaving breaths and beg for what I really want.

"Not like this. Your cock. I want to come on your cock. Please, I'm dying."

Shane grins unrepentantly. "No need to beg, sugar. Not yet anyway. We'll save that for later. Now stand up and lose those panties."

I jump off the bike and shed my undies at breakneck speed. While I work to get them off over my heels Shane is busy too. I look back up and she has her dick in her hand, stroking it slow and invitingly while she leans back against the handlebars. As I watch she pushes down, grinding the base against her clit. What a beautiful sight. I can't wait to see her face when she comes.

She stops me as I start to climb back on. "Normally I wouldn't do this." She pats the leather seat below her. "This is my baby, and I don't let just any woman on my bike. Mona said you were special. Don't make me regret my decision."

I shake my head. "I won't. Tell me what you want me to do and I'll do it."

Shane pats the seat again, this time in invitation. "Mmm, that's what I like to hear. Now climb up on top of my cock and show me how well you can ride. We'll work out the other details later at my place."

Later? There's going to be a later? I don't know what I did to deserve this, but I'm thankful all the same. Women like Shane are rare and I'm blessed to have found her.

We both know the ride is going to be short. We're too turned on for anything long and drawn out. This is just an appetizer.

She grips my rear and holds me suspended over her dick. "Are you wet?"

Wet? I'm fucking soaked, and I know she can see the evidence on my thighs even in the dark. I can definitely feel it. Lube at this point would just be redundant. "Oh yes. I'm drenched. Please, I need to fuck you."

Shane laughs, low and deep. "You may be on top, but I'm the one doing the fucking. I'm in control. Never forget that."

A true dominant to the core. Thank you, Jesus! "No Sir, I won't."

No further words are necessary. In one easy motion she lowers me onto her rod, slowly so as not to hurt me. The tenderness isn't necessary and I let her know it with my body as I writhe and buck for more. She takes the hint and drops me down the rest of the way in a quick flick of her wrists. I waste no time. Her hands are on my hips and my arms are around her shoulders, both of us pumping and working for the orgasm just within reach.

"That's it baby. Take it. Take it all. Good girl."

I'm cursing and praying and begging all at the same time like some naughty Catholic schoolgirl set loose on her first sexual adventure. I've never had it so good and the end is rapidly approaching. "Fuck, shit. Oh god. Right there. I'm about to come. Harder."

She lifts me up and manages mid-fuck to miraculously switch our positions. My back is against the handlebars now and my dress is around my waist. Shane is pumping her hips and fucking me like a marathon runner with her sights set on the finish line. I beat her there, but just barely. My fingernails are dug into her biceps and I'm screaming as I flood her cock with wetness. She grunts a few times and her body starts to shake as she reaches orgasm right after me. I was right. The look on her face as she comes is gorgeous.

We stay like that for a few minutes. My pussy is still clenching her dick with small aftershocks, the kind that come from only really good, rough sex. I'm whipped, sweaty and satisfied. I can't wait to hop back on the back of her Harley for the ride to her place.

"Oh, sweetheart. Mona was right. I'd be a fool to let you go. Wanna go for another ride?"

I know she means on the bike, because neither of us is in the shape to fuck again so soon. Shane withdraws slowly and helps me down. As she tucks herself back in I pull my panties back on. I wince as the adrenaline recedes and a slight throbbing of a different kind sets in. In my current state, the ride to her place is going to be interesting in more ways than one.

"You okay?"

I nod. "Just a bit sore, but I don't mind. I like a little pain sometimes."

Shane's eyes light up and her smile is positively evil. I'm instantly turned on again. I wonder if she is even more dominant than I first thought? I hope I'll find out once we make it to her house. I owe Mona more than a simple thank-you.

She revs the bike to life once more and pats the seat behind her. "Hop back on, sweetie. I've got plans for you. You can call Mona tomorrow from my house."

CHANNELING CHARLES BUKOWSKI

Aimee Herman

I put on a pair of loose corduroy pants so worn out that the velvety ribs no longer appear erect. I bind my breasts with a soft Ace bandage that suffocates my tits, causing my nipples to retreat inward, and put on a button-down dark brown shirt that hangs against me in a way that hides my curves and waist indentations. I put on a tie, but then decide against it. Charles wouldn't care enough to create a double-Windsor.

When everything has been buttoned, zipped, pulled on, or pressed against, I go into my sock drawer. I test out a combination of fabrics, lengths, and colors. Does it matter that my cock will be blue striped? The ones with yellow stars create a perfect length and width, but there is something strange about having gaseous spheres decorate my powerful new appendage. No. I decide to go with white cotton socks. Two inverted and folded together with another sock stuffed inside. I mold it and shape it, suddenly wondering if men had the secret wish to do the same with their cocks. Then I wonder if Charles was circumcised and how accurate I need to be with this costume.

I am channeling Charles Bukowski today on this yearly celebration of costumes and candy consumption. Halloween, my favorite day of the year. I have to be at work in an hour and I have two subways to catch, so I insert my dick into my underwear and allow the tight boy-shorts to digest its weight and size. I paint on a messy beard and mustache with eyeliner, making me appear as though I spent my morning French-kissing a subway platform, grab a cup of coffee and a dry piece of toast, and walk toward Franklin Avenue.

I don't expect much observance of Halloween in the office. I work at a marketing and PR firm, where I spend much of my time wondering what I actually do for a living—mostly sched-uling of lunch and dinner meetings, retrieving messages and e-mails, and the creation of spreadsheets.

Charlotte in HR is dressed as Strawberry Shortcake or a redheaded maid; I'm not quite sure. Dave from accounting is a baseball player. There are three witches, a bloody doctor, many sexy nurses, an astronaut, and various burn victims, one-armed ghouls, and convicts. No one seems to know who I am.

"Charles Bukowski? Was he the guy that had that cult in the nineties? Telling everyone to kill each other and have sex with him?"

"No."

"Was he vice president when Reagan was in office?"

"Are you kidding me?"

I walk toward my desk when Charlotte struts toward me. Charlotte, pre-Halloween, is quite nondescript. She is kind of like an unsharpened pencil, dull and light.

"I've always been more into his stories than his poetry," she says.

"Finally, someone who knows who I am."

"Great facial hair," she adds, though I swear she is looking down to where my cotton cock protrudes.

As my day progresses, I notice something remarkable about my costume: Every time I shift in my seat, adjust the posture of my legs, or straighten my back, my cock moves and presses deeper against my clit. It is a marvelous sensation. I get up to refill my coffee mug and feel it again, only heightened. With each step, my cock becomes animated, rubbing up against my clit, getting raw from the friction and hard from the attention. I leave my mug in the employee kitchen and retreat to the bathroom.

I hesitate at the door signs. Technically, I am a man today, a man who spent his days drinking poetry, booze, and women. Don't I have the right to use the men's room today? I've always wanted to try peeing standing up. I did it once in college, but I was extremely drunk and wound up creating a very embarrassing moment for myself.

My hands push open the door and I walk in. I expect walls covered in graffiti and naked women taped beside each stall, loud, boisterous half-naked men slapping each other and sucking each other's cocks.

The bathroom is empty, creating a rush of disappointment. Everything looks the same, except of course, for the urinals. I want to be adventurous, but instead I choose a stall. I unbuckle my belt, unzip my pants, and let them fall to my ankles. I stare at my black underwear creating a new shape. Standing against the wall, I spread my legs a little, bringing my hand to where my cock hides, contained by cotton and elastic. I give myself a hand job, pressing it against my cunt. It is widest at the tip, not very long, but I imagine the way it would feel running into me like an elevator plummeting down. The force of impact. The repetition of in-and-out motion.

The fabric against my pubic hairs causes a tingly sensation, different than usual. Uncomfortable, but a good discomfort, like being punished with hard sex and a time-out ending in finger-nail screams and volatile ejaculations. I take a deep breath, but continue my exploration. I want to wrap my absorbent white dick inside a fist of skin and straddle it. My breasts are sweating beneath the binding and I push out my chest to create friction for my nipples. The sensations are new and angry and on fire. The motion of dick against clit and finger shaking, pushing into me, swells my breaths and makes me unable to stop what I am doing. I can feel myself getting very close to—

I hear the bathroom door open. Hard footsteps create a clacking sound. I peek through the crack left between door and frame, surprised to see Emily, who is almost unrecognizable today in leather fringe, holster, and complete cow*boy* getup. Emily and I have barely acknowledged each other in the past, except for holiday parties or occasional inter-office meetings. She works in accounting and rarely makes contact with non-number crunchers. On a regular workday, she dresses in identifiable femme wear: Calves are pushed high up toward her thighs in four-inch skinny heels; stockings slide tightly over her legs, creating a mirage of shimmered length or a long seam that extends all the way up. Her hair, which is dark chocolate and wavy, is generally worn down. It is wild at times, depending upon weather, and slams against her shoulders when she walks. She wears just enough makeup to still allow a glimpse into her natural skin tone, lip structure and eyes. Her lips are often painted pale red, pomegranate red, poppy red. Her lashes can be admired from across any size room. I bet she uses one of those odd lash-curling contraptions; I had a lover once who used to swear by those things, torturing her lashes several times a day by squeezing them between metal. Okay, so I've noticed her.

It appears her curiosities match mine. The impact of her

buckles and snaps echo against the dirty concrete flooring of the bathroom. I watch as she investigates her almost unrecognizable reflection in the large wall-extended mirror.

I take a deep breath and do my best to remain focused on my own activities within the cramped stall, though I immediately become unhinged when I sense Emily's footsteps coming toward the door separating us.

"Is someone in here?" she asks, her voice disrupting the hard stretched leather theme of her costume.

"Uhhh," is all I can say. I hold on tightly to my dick and remain focused with two fingers firmly inside.

She wastes no time guessing as she peeks between the cracks of the stall and grabs onto my stare.

"Charles Bukowski," she says. "You think Charles ever did it with a cowboy?"

I smile and attempt laughter, then realize I am in an extremely compromising and potentially job-removing position.

"You gonna let me in?"

It is in this moment that I must make the most important decision of my day: remove fingers from inside me or unwrap palm from cotton cock. Decisions, decisions.

I disconnect from my dick and unlatch the door with my free hand, deciding to once again channel Charles and do exactly what he would have done. Act by cock alone, don't ask questions, and take what I can get. There is barely enough room for me in here; I can't imagine how all of her tassels and leather will fit.

"I kind of expected something different in here," Emily says, "but it's just like *our* bathroom, only with different smells."

There is a brief moment of awkwardness.

"You on a break?" I ask.

"No, but I can take one. This can replace the time I might

take to walk outside and smoke a cigarette. I've been trying to quit anyway."

She takes off her cowboy hat and places it on the hook against the door. There is no choice but to press our impressively bony hips against each other. Her breasts push out the flannel buttons on her shirt and I have no guilt as I blatantly study their hidden shape and size. Emily stares into me as she lifts each button through its slot and forces my imagination to stop. They are shocked by their release and immediately shudder. Burnt pink nipples grow swollen and pointy. Her belly is flat with a subtle looseness that reveals more of an interest in sex than sit-ups. I want to lick all that leather off her skin. She pulls my head toward her tits and I suck like a man, like a well-trained butch because today I am both. My teeth tease her pain capacity, and she appears to be the type to have a high threshold.

My cock is dangling from the slot in my underwear. She takes advantage of this magical holiday and presses her cowskinned knees against the ground. I can't believe this. My first day with a cock and I am already getting a blow job. No wonder guys cannot focus with a dick in their pants; it's like a quarter found between couch cushions or an all-you-can-eat free buffet. No one can resist.

She puts her naked lips over my cotton-socked cock. I can feel her breath peer into the rest of me. Her distinctive smell pushes against my thighs, and I can sense the natural aroma of her pores and herbal shampoo in her hair. The sounds she is making are unreal—a blend of monkey moans and paper-jam fax machine trouble. There is a moment of worry that the thick cotton will clog up her throat and sop up all the wetness stored in her mouth. Emily grabs my hand, which had been penetrating my cunt, and moves it toward her face. She rams her tongue between my fingers and sucks on the juices.

"Emily, I—"

She bites down on my finger and sucks away a layer of my fingerprints.

Then she grabs my cock and presses it hard into my pubic hair and bone. The pressure feels extremely satisfying. She pushes down the underwear housing my new appendage, and I watch as it falls to the floor. I immediately feel sadness as my cock hits the dirty ground, but it is washed away the moment Emily slides her tongue between my pussy lips, then takes turns nibbling and swatting at my folds. Up until now, I had never let a girl go there, minus a few times in college. I am a top, wrist-grabber, dominant thruster. Allowing anyone down there in this way puts me in too vulnerable a position. But I'm not me today; I'm not political butch bull dyke; I am a man who was too boozed up and covered in poems to say no or have a *type*, so I just let go.

Suddenly, I understand what it feels like to be bisexual—the best of *both* worlds—except my genitals are sexual multitaskers, transforming shape and desire. My dick wants to be sucked on, to stick itself into something, *someone*. My pussy wants to be stuffed, filled, suffocated.

Emily is bobbing for apples, or maybe just my orgasm, which she seems to realize she has interrupted. As her tongue darts in and out of me, mixing her spit with my own extract, I reach behind me and grab the flask resting in my back pocket. It is part of my costume (if anyone asks). But, it is also full of whiskey, coming in handy at this very moment.

I unscrew the cap and take a swig. Emily speaks something into my cunt that sounds like a question, but all that matters is the whir of her letters mashing together, causing a vibration to steam me open even farther. I let the whiskey burn my gums, before grabbing Emily's head, bringing it to my face, and letting the liquor fall into her mouth. She gags, unprepared for the sting, and bends back down, raining the liquor over and into my pussy. The rest of me feels drunk. Why not forcefully inebriate my cunt too?

Everything is opening up, contracting and moistening. My cunt shakes with every tongue thrust and fat finger insertion, curving like commas, slithering like bendable snakes. I slam my shoulders into the hard wall behind me and scream, pressing my thighs into Emily's face, asphyxiating her hearing capacity.

Suddenly the bathroom door opens again. Fuck. Why didn't I lock the door? I am so close, *so close*, right there, and now I have to be quiet again. She has to stop. I cannot—

"Shh," she whispers inside me.

There is a flush, the sound of the bathroom door opening and footsteps walking out. No hand washing. Neither of us seem to mind.

Then Emily slowly pulls down her zipper, revealing cloudy blue panties with a giant wet spot. I can smell how turned on she is and I am desperate to taste it. She wiggles out of her leather and panties and I notice how smooth her thighs are in comparison to my hairy ones. Her cunt is manicured and contained by an octagon-like bush compared to my wild, uninhibited one. If my dick were real, could get hard, fill with semen, I'd waste no time exercising it inside her. With proper protection, of course. But I am without an external tool, so I am forced to improvise.

I press my four fingers together tightly, like a huddle of football players ready to make the most important play of their lives. I place my wrist up against my pubic bone and reveal my DIY erection. She smiles, appreciative of my creative inventiveness. I sling it inside her wet pussy as though it is in the shape of a lasso literally pulling her in. She curves her hips against me, working her way toward my knuckles. Her weight presses into me; my bandaged breasts; my saturated pubic hair. We smell of whiskey and leather and all the juices that have rushed out.

It begins.

A heat that rises from within every pore and angle. Cuticles. Ankles. Behind the knees. Where scars come from. The space between top lip and nostrils. Earlobes. Roots and ends of hair. Collarbone. Hips. Anus. Belly button.

Words are screamed out that have not yet made their way into the English-language dictionaries. Emily rips at my shoulder blades and practically punctures my eardrums with high-decibel screams. We remain in that stall for a few minutes longer to gain composure and a safe breathing pattern.

She kisses the sweat-smeared beard and mustache off my skin. I am so turned on by her blurred identity that I want to do it again. Even though I have no energy. Even though I have probably been in here the span of two lunch breaks. I hold on to her hips and breathe her in. Her hair has rebelliously fled from its tight ponytail, so I take the opportunity to run my dirty fingers in her melted chocolate locks. Though back in her cowboy costume, I now see what hides beneath. The softness. Graceful curvature. The swell of her breasts and flexibility of her nipples. In the space of this bathroom stall there is no room for tag names or distinctive identifications. We are bodies, bled into each other. Our parts, limbs, groins change and shift. I can dominate and *be* dominated.

Emily lets go of my bottom lip, which she has been concentrating on, grabs her hat, and begins to turn the latch of the door. I swat her ass in a playful way as she walks out. I am unsure of how long I've been in this bathroom, but I decide to remain. I pick up my flaccid white dick from the floor and dust it off. I remove its outer sock shell and reconfigure its shape and size. It is thinner now and definitely not as impressive. I wait for the door to swing open again.

TITS DOWN, ASS UP

Crystal Barela

W here the fuck have you been, Cali?" Tony's deep voice was muffled by how close he was bent over the chick in front of him. He needed glasses, and I swear he didn't get them so he had an excuse to lean in close and work his fetish for women's perfumes.

"Traffic," I said. The back door shut behind me and I threw my gear in the corner. I ran my hands through my short straight black hair so it stood on end.

"Shit, kid," he said. "Why don't you take the subway like the rest of the East Village?"

My wheels were pulled up in the alley behind the shop. The Softail with shiny chrome rims was the perfect reason for braving the streets of Manhattan. "Reputation."

Tony snorted and said, "That one's been waiting on you for more than an hour." He gestured with his head to the front of the shop.

There were half a dozen girls sitting on the shiny red vinyl in front of our shop window. Their tattooed backs and shoulders were the perfect draw for the curious window shoppers cruising by on the sidewalk out front.

"Lucy, who's my first victim?" Our receptionist—I nearly laughed out loud at the formality of the title given to our single employee. She had taken the position for the free tats and the steady flow of ladies visiting the shop for my artistic attention.

"Tantra!" Lucy called out, as if our customers weren't mere feet from her desk.

Was that name for real? I scanned the ladies, clicking the bar in my tongue against the back of my teeth. A nasty habit that I found to be a turn-off in other women, but I somehow derived great pleasure in doing myself.

"Tantra?" I called in a friendlier invite.

No answer. Not everyone believed in fashionably late like I did.

The shop was silent when I opened the door the next morning. Truth was, I hadn't gone to sleep the night before. Some might say that I shouldn't be poking people with sharp objects then, but personally I thought a little overtime in the waking world made me more attuned.

Besides, Tony was in DC. His old lady's kid was graduating from college. Marco was flying in from El Paso that afternoon to keep the empty chair filled for the next two weeks.

I flipped on the lights. The mirrored wall that ran the length of the shop was framed by thick red velvet drapes. The other walls were black and decorated with photos of all of our celebrity clients.

I paused in front of the picture of me and Jolie. Now those were some motherfucking hot lips. If I do recall, I thought, rocking back on the heels of my black leather boots, we'd held more than each other's hands. Shit! Don't believe me? This was before Brad, and truth be told, before Billy Bob. I'd only been eighteen at the time. Barely legal. I was Tony's apprentice then and only able to touch her skin with my fingers. No matter how I had pleaded, Tony had not let me hold a needle.

I sat into the overstuffed chair, set my boots on the desk, and crossed my feet at the ankles. Lucy would try to kick my ass if she knew. She hadn't come to the realization that this wasn't her shop.

The first client under my name on Lucy's clipboard: Tantra. There couldn't be another woman with that name, even in Manhattan. Midweek was usually slow and the mysterious Tantra was due—

The bells on the door chimed and I let the clipboard rest against my forehead, hiding in a few more seconds of silence. She was early.

"Cali! Baby!" Marco tilted back on the heels of his cowboy boots and held out his arms.

I hopped over the desk and flew into his chest. I nearly knocked him off his feet. He pounded my back.

"You smell awesome," I said. A musky cologne.

"Cigarettes," he said with a sniff, not loosening his hold. "No time to go home and shower?"

"Fuck," I said. "No time to be a gentleman?"

"Remember who you're talking to, brotha." Marco leaned back and peered down at me with the devil's eyes. "Is she done?"

"Thirty-nine hours." I undid the button fly of my Levi's and tugged the hem of my black tee to my braless breasts.

Koi. The Japanese consider them a symbol of energy and power. Chris O'Donnell, a genius with the needle, had tattooed the one swimming from between my legs. The length of the fish's body wrapped around my hip, circled my waist, and reappeared under my arm, the lips stopping to feed at my right breast. This masterpiece of color and grace had taken more than a year to complete with my shitty schedule and Chris's shop being in LA. Marco had seen the design before he left for home last year.

"Brilliant."

"I know," I said, running a hand down my rib cage. "I wish I could work naked."

Marco laughed. "Me too."

"Are you Cali?" Her voice was lush. Wet. My imagination sent my pussy swimming.

"Shop closes at midnight," I called out from the back of the shop, regret in my voice. My back was to the door as I stuffed my face with a hot dog Marco had brought back from the street vendor. It was cold from earlier this evening, but there is nothing like a New York City frank.

"That's not what the sign says," she called back.

That voice. I wiped my mouth with a napkin. "Look, honey, Marco is gonna be here in the morning."

"No, I want you to do me."

The way she said it made my insides burn.

I turned.

Where I was lanky and all limbs, she was hips and thighs. I topped her by a good five inches. Her ass was in abundance and painted into her jeans. Her eyes were that somewhere between blue and green only found in nature, fringed with reddish blond lashes, and looking at me like she could eat me up.

She took my hand, her sleeveless arm pale and bare of color. Her fingers were decorated in large chunky rings of jewel-colored cut glass.

"Maybe I could make an exception for...?" Was there a discreet way to check my breath for lingering hot-dog odors?

"Tantra."

"It's you."

She laughed. "It's me."

I took her hand. "I've been expecting you for about two weeks now."

"Nerves."

"A virgin?"

She raised an eyebrow and her lips twitched.

"Your skin, it's bare? A virgin to the needle?"

"Yes, no tattoos."

"Well then, you've come to the right place," I said, leading her over to my chair.

At the back of the shop I had the sketch she'd left last week on one of her many no-shows. I had thought twice about working on the transfer, considering Tantra's track record of making appointments and breaking them, but it was an inspiring drawing. It had honestly been a turn-on to spend some time with the sketch.

I had done a tree of life before, but not of this size. The roots twisted into a Celtic circle pattern at the base and the trunk of the tree rose in a knotty line, its branches curling out to the sides about six inches up. Leaves clung to the branches. It was really quite beautiful. Expensive and time-consuming too. It had been designed for a woman's back.

"Turn around, baby."

As she turned, Tantra lifted her shirt up over her head. God, I love my job! I got a quick peek at her full, round breasts, tucked into black lace bra cups. This was one ripe woman. Hot.

"You know the lower back is one of the most painful places for a woman to get a tattoo?"

"Yes." There was a thrill in her voice.

"And that this is gonna take at least three sittings?"

"You can't do it all tonight?"

"It's an eight-hour job."

"I'd pay extra."

"You want color too?"

Tantra nodded. I walked toward the back of the shop, sketch in hand. The leaves on the branches were so delicate, gold and green. They seemed to move as if a breeze were blowing in the background.

Was I actually considering this? I hadn't slept in more than twenty-four hours, and this wasn't an easy job. I rubbed the back of my neck and looked down at Tantra, clutching her shirt beneath her beautiful breasts, the bits of lace not hiding the shadows of her nipples. She was worrying her lower lip with her teeth. One tooth was crooked. Sexy.

I patted the black vinyl of my chair and she hopped on board, her feet dangling in cute espadrille wedge sandals.

"Why is this tattoo important to you, honey?" Tantra's back was to me. I unhooked her bra. She sucked in her breath as I lifted her thick red curls from her shoulders and secured them with a hair clip on top of her head.

"My sister, she drew this," she whispered in that sultry voice. "We're twins."

If that didn't put a wet spot in my jeans.

"In a couple of months I'm going to see her in Ireland."

"Unzip your jeans." The drag of the zipper and a shimmy of hips revealed the white of her skin to the crack of her ass. Was she wearing panties?

I covered my palms with shave oil and spread it over Tantra's shoulder blades. Her skin was pale and smooth, except for where her bra had left red lines. I lingered a bit too long, massaging the marks away. She sighed, and I found I was in danger of losing my professionalism.

The crinkle of the plastic being torn from the razor and then the smooth swipe of blade across her opalescent skin made my lips ache. Gently, I laid the transfer on her back and then wet it with a sponge, dabbing at the smooth canvas of her back. I lifted a corner of the paper and drew it across her back.

A sigh tinged with sex filled my shop as I pulled the paper free.

Looked good. Too good. I handed the mirror over her shoulder and pointed her in the direction of the wall. "Check the placement, sugar." Get a grip, Cali. Work before pleasure.

Tantra went over to the mirrored wall and held up the hand mirror to look over her shoulder. "Perfect!" she squealed, with a little hop. She turned to the right, then left, and all my eyes saw were her breasts, now bare and free. Nipples puckered from the night air coming through the back door teased me.

I rubbed my eyes. Tired and horny, that's what I was.

"Tantra, baby, I think we should reschedule." Sleep would help me to concentrate on my art and not her ass.

"No!" She bounced over to me and took my hands in hers.

"I haven't slept in days and—"

She put my hands on her tits, and the thought of putting her off was gone.

"Another night won't hurt."

"You have a point," I said, massaging her breasts. I leaned down, her face nearing mine.

A kiss, two nips.

Shook my head, took a step back. "Okay, beautiful," I said. "Tits down, ass up."

Silent tears were running down Tantra's face, which belied the soft sighs and moans that escaped each pass of my tattoo gun. She was one of those that liked the pain, and although I was known to have a gentle hand, she didn't want it. I was surprised she wasn't covered in tats and piercings.

With every gasp I had to force myself not to throw my tattoo gun aside and fuck her. The scent of her arousal was driving me mad.

"Nearly done, baby," I said. A lie to myself. I had finished the Celtic knot and still had the entire tree to do. The goal was to finish the outline tonight. We were only a half hour in. I wiped my brow, bent and adjusted the knob on my tattoo machine. I was a professional.

Tantra gave her ass a wiggle, pressing her pussy into the vinyl. "More, Cali," she pleaded.

Not gonna make it. "Be still, sugar." My voice was harsh, my throat dry.

I sprayed the inky skin with water and wiped it with the towel, now discolored with black ink. I spread Vaseline across the tat. Looked good.

"Why'd you want me to do you?" I asked.

Wipe, spray, tat.

"Charlotte Scott."

My hand wavered. Charlotte? Charlotte had a thing for pain too. More than the little buzz my gun produced.

Wipe, spray, tat.

Her ass had been in the exact same spot as Tantra's pussy. Three in the morning. Clothing optional. I'd worn nothing but a strap-on. Nearly fucked Charlott's pussy raw, right after piercing her clit. Now that's pain.

"You trying to tell me something, sugar?" I drew my hand along the small of her back, the trunk of the tree taking shape.

"Breathe deep," Tantra said. "Smell that?"

"My pussy's been hot for you since Charlotte told me how she got her piercing."

I placed a hand on the small of her back. "Suck it up, darlin'," I said.

Tantra looked over her shoulder and caught my eyes.

"No."

Oh shit.

"I am so wet."

Oh fuck. I closed my eyes trying to find my strength of will. "What do you want more, sugar?" I whispered. "This tattoo or my face in your pussy?"

Tantra stood and turned around, hooking her thumbs in the waistband of her jeans. The jeans shimmied down her thighs and I holstered my gun. She kicked the jeans aside.

My smooth moves were out the door. All I could think of was tasting every inch of her body. Her lips were plump and sweet. Her neck soap-scented. I buried my face between her breasts, nosing around like an animal. The sweat where the soft mounds met her body was salty and bold.

My synthetic-gloved fingers slipped through her sopping slit. One, two fingers found a home in her hot hole. I forced her back onto the table, sure to press her tat into the vinyl. She cried out, but her pussy squeezed my fingers.

Tantra clutched my head to her breasts and I devoured her hard nipples. Biting, bruising suction. Her hips bucked and she urged me lower.

I nibbled my way over her soft round stomach, past her belly button, and into the thick curly hair covering her snatch. Her swollen pussy lips glistened.

My hand pinned her to the tattooing chair. My fingers dove in and out, piercing her hungry hole. Her lips became redder and the skin around her thighs flushed.

My tongue circled her clit. A third finger wedged its way into her hungry cunt.

She panted, pushing her hips against me.

The muscles in her thighs squeezed my cheeks.

My tongue bar gave her a kiss.

Fingers yanked my hair.

Tantra screamed.

Tears wet her cheeks as her pussy bathed my face.

Sweet Jesus. I pulled my bruised fingers free and sat back on my heels. I undid my fly. Just a couple of strokes and I'd be with her.

"No," she gasped.

I froze. Not sure I was ready to take orders yet. I just wanted to get off.

"Stand."

I did, and my jeans fell to my ankles. My cunt pulsed.

"Take off your shirt."

I lifted the hem of my tee and watched her come to me on wobbly legs.

"So beautiful," she said. Tantra traced a finger from the mouth of the koi sucking my breast. She followed the orange and gold scales around my torso. Her lips repainted the bold lines of the graceful fins on my shoulder blades with soft kisses and wet licks. They followed the curling trail of ink between my legs and set me free.

Tantra tapped my clit, then plunged her tongue into my folds, releasing my koi. The fish burst from my skin and into the air, swimming in circles around my head as I came in dizzying waves.

Tantra stood and then laid her body tits down on the chair, her beautiful ass bare.

I buttoned my fly and picked up a fresh white rag. The work I had done earlier was bleeding and the skin red.

"I'm sorry, sugar," I said.

"Didn't feel a thing."

I placed a tender kiss on the abused flesh at the base of her spine and promised myself I would stop thinking about pussy.

Tantra sucked in her breath and I squeezed my thighs together.

I sprayed her skin with water and washed the smooth flesh carefully before turning on my tattoo machine.

"Ready for a rough ride, baby?"

"You promise to kiss it all better?"

The ache she had just eased began to spread through my lower body. "And then some."

POUND

Shanna Germain

You can tell a lot about how a woman fucks by the stray she takes home.

I know, you don't believe me. I'm not ashamed to say I'm a girl who's done her research. Some of it's secondhand, of course—a girl can't be that busy all the time, even if she'd like to be. But between me and YoYo—that's Yolanda for those who don't know her well—we've got the map pretty much covered.

We sit at the pound all day long, and we watch the pretty girls walk in, looking for a companion to take home. There are two girls in the dog room now, walking between the cages. One has a boy on her arm, and they're doing the baby cooing noises that couples tend to do. The other is quite a bit older, maybe YoYo's age, though she'd deny it, stalking the cages, looking at the medium-sized dogs, namely a brownish mutt and a golden cocker spaniel. YoYo and I already have a bet going that she'll be taking the cocker home.

See, here's what we've figured out so far. Any woman who

looks at the yappers—you know, those little dogs that'd bite your ankle as soon as look at it, she's a nothing in the sack. Mind you, I love all the dogs—it's my job—but there are some I love a whole lot more than others. A girl takes one of those little things, especially if she just happens to have a pink collar in her bag to wrap around the poor creature's scrawny little neck, and you know she's a priss fuck. The kind that'll tease you with her little wiggling ass in a skirt, bend over the desk to show her tits, but who won't want to get all down and dirty, no way. The kind that'll have a meltdown if you mess with her hair.

YoYo likes those ones. Says she likes to push them over the edge, see if she can make them crack. "It's all about cunny, Kay," YoYo says, sticking her tongue between her thick fingers like some teenage boy. "You just gotta know how to eat it, and a girl who's wailing about her broken nail one second will be begging you to paddle her ass raw the next." I trust YoYo in most things girl, but that, I don't buy. Not for one second.

Now, slobbery breeds like boxers and bulldogs—a girl goes for one of them and you know she's the wild kind. Doesn't care about getting down and dirty. She'll muck you up and get mucked up and not even blink twice. I like dirty, but that's too dirty for me. Not the fucking, never that, but those are the girls with couches full of dog hair and cars that stink of ciga-rette butts and old pizza; girls who are still wearing yesterday's undies and last year's lover's shirt. Pass. Nuh-uh, not for me.

I like the ones who appreciate big, clean dogs. Nothing too hyper. Dalmatians are out. High-bred papered pretties that can't so much as figure out how to pee without help? Out. And mean dogs are not an option—all those girls who pick breeds like pit bulls, just for sake of saying they have a pit bull.

Now, girls who pick Labs, those are good. German shep-herds. Huskies. The mixes. Smart, calm dogs with a fine spirit in their eyes. Intelligent enough to disarm you. The ones that will know their own pleasure and want to discover yours. They're the ones who will pull out a strap-on, or surprise you by knowing how to breathe and let you open them up around your fist. Or they do this flutter thing with their tongue that will make you arch and scream. They're the ones I like.

YoYo elbows me as the front door opens, and I turn, trying not to gape. This new one is dressed in a camel-colored dress and sweater set. Camel-colored boots that hug her calves and show off the dimples at the curves of her knees. Long, straight dark hair with bangs cut short across the front. Sounds girlish, right? I think so. Too high-maintenance. All that perfection.

I suddenly feel self-conscious in my dog-hair-coated jeans and my *Give An Animal a Home* T-shirt, my short hair sticking up like it always does when I've been wrestling with the pups.

The new woman gives us both a smile, pale lips that are almost frosted. Her face is round and clear, and looks like those magazine ads from when I was little, cherry ChapStick and snow-pinked lips and a cute little hat pulled down to show off her eyes. For the longest time, I thought I wanted to be one of those girls, took me far too long to realize I wanted to be *with* one of those girls.

"Okay to just browse?" the woman asks. She seems nervous, a little hesitant, which is kind of endearing inside all that glamour.

I open and close my mouth, pretty sure I said something. Maybe it was just a squeak.

"Yeah, please," YoYo says. "It's what we're here for." YoYo's one of those women who can say just about anything and get away with it as long as she says it in that soft tone of voice of hers. It's no wonder the animals love her.

While the new girl is walking up through the cages, I take bets with YoYo that she'll take a teacup. Some shivering creature small enough to fit in a handbag. Priss, through and through. Which doesn't explain why I can't get the image out of my head: throwing her down on my couch, tussling up that perfect hair, pushing that perfect skirt up around her waist.

"Twenty-five on that," YoYo says. We bet in cents, not dollars. YoYo lost five bucks to me once too often and kicked the price down. "Can't afford to be buying you your soy latte caramel whatevers every day. It's black cuppa or nothing," she said.

We both just like to bet, I think. And YoYo's getting good at the signs. On this one she takes the bet, shaking her head. "Check out the legs. She works out. And the nails. Natural. She's gonna go for a big boy. Something protective for her walks."

Damn. I didn't even notice the nails.

I watch the girl walk between the cages—she's got fine, muscular legs that show in the space between the hem of her short dress and her calf-high boots. When she squats down to look at the dogs, the muscles slide beneath the skin and I don't mean to, but I inhale in an audible gasp.

"Mmm-mmm," YoYo says, eyeing me to let me know she heard. "She is yummy."

I have to agree. Despite her made-upness, there's something natural and athletic about her that appeals.

"I'm gonna go help her pick her guard dog," YoYo says, laughing as she pushes her chair back. "See if I can't win both a girl and a bet in one shot."

"You do that," I call. YoYo looks back at me, curls her fingers into a circle. It could be the shape of a quarter. It could be the sign for winning. It could be an O for orgasm. Knowing YoYo, it's all three.

* * *

The couple leaves without choosing anything, and I bet myself they're going to be having the dog versus baby discussion in the car. You could tell from her eyes that she wants both and he isn't sure he wants either. I lay a quarter on YoYo's keyboard—I originally thought they'd take a puppy for sure. YoYo's still in with the woman and the dogs. They're talking, but it's hard to make out what they're saying from here. Not sure I want to anyway. I like YoYo, she's one of those rare coworkers who became a friend, but I don't really know if I want to hear all her pickup lines.

The older woman comes out bearing the cocker's card in her hand. She says she wants to adopt, which is a moment I truly love, and I give her all the necessary paperwork to fill out. Adopting a pet's not like it used to be, when you just needed to point and pay. Too many got returned. So now we need a shitload of information, including the phone of the landlord, just to make sure that it really is written in the lease that pets are allowed. I take my quarter back after she leaves. Now the gamble is Even Steven, as YoYo would say.

Now we're just waiting on the girl to see which way the betting tips.

I let my gaze slide over to her and YoYo inside the kennels, and I realize that although YoYo's talking to her and she's nodding, her eyes are watching me through the glass. We have barely a moment to connect—just long enough for me to see that her eyes are as black as her hair—and then she returns her gaze to the dogs in front of her.

A few minutes later, YoYo comes back into the office, grinning ear to ear, tsking her tongue to the roof of her mouth. "She wants you," she says.

"Fuck she does," I say.

"No, I mean it. She has some questions about Roxie," she says. Roxie's a bull terrier crossed with who knows what. Maybe pit bull, maybe some kind of lab. All white, but for a couple of black spots on his ears, and without the Roman nose you usually find in purebreds.

YoYo's still grinning at me. "I told her you were our expert resident in smart dogs," she says. "'Sides, she's not my type."

"Turned you down, did she?" I ask. I tap the quarter with my nail. I feel stupidly giddy, and my grin just won't settle down.

"Not hardly, honey," YoYo says, as she sits. "No one ever turns me down." She picks up the quarter from beside my keyboard, plays it through her fingers with a laugh. "Now go talk to the girl. It's almost five o'clock. I'll start closing up."

I go in and am instantly surrounded by the din of barks and whines and soft keens. I'd never say this to YoYo, but sometimes working here kills me. I want to take every one of these dogs home and show them that they're loved. But of course, you can only do so much. And my so much, at the moment, especially since I live in an apartment, is working here.

Girls are different. I don't want to take any of them home. I might go home with them, let them host me and fuck me. And then I trot off in the early morning hours, like a stray who's slipped her collar and needs to remember the way freedom feels as it rushes past her ears.

The girl's down on her haunches inside Roxie's cage, letting Roxie lick her fingers and the fronts of her knees. I am suddenly jealous. I want to be the one to do that. I want to taste the pale curve of her legs, that heated stretch of skin on the inside of her thighs.

She has gorgeous hands—clean and natural, but strong too, like someone who could really hold a leash, like someone who could use them in other ways. And her legs, well, I've already drooled on about those. I'm worse than a dog with a bit of meat in front of her nose.

"Hey," I say as I open the door and step inside, swallowing away the soft tremor that seems to have taken over my voice. I can't help the way my eyes trace the soft curves of her body, the bent knees, the way her ass sings inside her skirt. "YoY-Yolanda said you had some questions? About Rox?"

She looks up at me, tilting her head. There's a tiny dimple in her chin that crinkles when she smiles. And a tiny pinpoint of a mole beneath one dark eye. Her face isn't standard pretty, not the way I first thought—too square, too pointed—but it's handsome, and her upturned gaze knocks me back, so hard that my breath is stilled in my chest.

"He's gorgeous," she says, in this kind of dreamy voice that reminds me of girls talking about boys. I can't tell if I like the sound of it or not. Roxie whines and sits, tail thumping against the wall of his cage, as though he knows she's talking about him. I'm sure, somehow, that he does.

Then the girl opens her mouth and laughs. She has a fantastic laugh, the kind that makes you want to laugh right along with her, even if you don't know what's funny.

"He is gorgeous," I say. "Smart too."

"Smart is important to me," she says, casting a glance back at Rox as she stands, brushing a hand down the front of her dress.

"He's gonna shed to hell on your camel-hair dress, though." It's not really camel-hair. Of course it's not. I can't believe I just said that out loud. I raise a hand, push my hair back out of my face, which has suddenly flared hot.

She looks down at herself, laughing again. The sound makes me feel slightly less stupid, but not much. I never get like this over a girl, all goopy. I'm a bet-on-'em, fuck-'em-and-leave-'em kind of girl. And yet I feel like a schoolgirl tripping over her own feet.

"It's just a dress," she says, like she means it. "I buy every-thing used anyway. And never, ever anything that has to be dry-cleaned. No way. I've had big dogs forever."

"Oh, well, then..." Brilliant. I swear, if I could put two words together, I would promise to never bet again.

She slides a hand forward and mine takes it. Her touch is warm and a little dog-hair coated, but I'm sure mine is too. "Marnie," she says.

"I'm Kay." I've never been so grateful to remember my own name.

"So, Kay," she says, and then she waits, still holding my hand. It's not like I'm supposed to say something in return. It's more like she's savoring the sound of my name, and the silence that comes after. There's the sound of our breathing, and Roxie's pant as he takes a seat on his haunches, looking back and forth at the two of us.

Another heartbeat high in my throat, another pant from Roxie, and a whine, and then she finishes. "What do I need to do if I want to take such a gorgeous, smart, strong creature home with me?"

The air is hot, swirling about me, dizzying my brain, sucking all the moisture from my tongue. The sound of my swallow is audible. Click.

"You would, um, you would have to fill out some paperwork. Get checked for your living situation and uh..." I can't for the fuck of me remember the rest. *Something something something* is what my brain is saying between heartbeats. And most of those heartbeats seem to be going straight to the space between my thighs, hammering and whining for attention.

I realize Marnie still has my hand. That her silver-ringed

thumb is sliding across my life line. I want to know what those fingers would feel like inside me, or tangled in my hair, or catching the point of my nipples between them.

"That seems doable," she says, and I wonder how she's able to talk so easily, when I can barely seem to find one word to follow another. Her dark eyes are ringed with even darker lashes, thick and sweeping, nearly brushing her cheeks as she half closes them, watching me through the sweep. "And how do I take the dog home?"

Now I really do stutter. Lost for words. Where are they? All tangled up in the leash of my tongue, caught in the collar of my throat.

Marnie leans in and touches her lips to mine, sucks in my breath as though she's trying to pull forth the missing words, to undo the knots and kinks that she's twisted my thoughts into. Her breath is sweet and spiced like sugared coffee and dark chocolate, and I lean into her touch with a sound that's more like a whine than anything else. In response, Roxie's tail thumps against the floor of his cage.

The sound causes Marnie to pull back and she laughs again. The laugh almost makes up for the fact that she's no longer touching me, that my lips are coated in lip gloss and the scent of her.

"You're a rare breed, women like you, Kay," she says.

"Oh?" It's kind of a question and kind of the only sound my mouth will make.

"Strong." Her hand up my arm as she speaks, resting on my bicep, which I seriously have to resist the urge to tighten. "Smart." The hand at the corner of my cheek, sweeping. "But a little soft on the inside, big puppy eyes and big puppy heart."

"I don't—" I start to say, even though I have no idea how I'm going to finish that sentence. It's a good thing she leans in and puts her lips on mine again, brushes that caramel-colored skirt against the front of my jeans. I don't even know I'm wet until she reaches a hand between our rolling hips, pushing the damp fabric of my underwear against my skin.

Now she's all sweet and tart, like cotton candy and lemonade. So many layers, and I want to taste them all. I know that YoYo's out there somewhere, a full view of this through the glass, I know there's a slim chance that someone will walk in just before closing time and see us here, bodies entwined in the pound, but it's a distant knowing, far away, like an alarm clock you can barely hear through a fantastic dream.

"Mmm, fuck," I breathe against her mouth.

"Yes, please," is what she says, a husk in her voice, and her blatant want—sweet desire, combined with words that are nothing short of a command—knocks me over. I slide down on my knees in front of her, like she's something to worship, and maybe she is. My fingers run up those legs, soft skin, hard muscle, pushing the hem of the skirt up. She shifts, opening her thighs to let me in.

There is nothing under her camel skirt except her skin, close shaved, her lips parting for my mouth, her heat spilling over my liquid in an instant flood of warmth. I lick her, soft, barely touching. Her hips slide against me, echoing the catch and release of her breath. She is creamy on the inside, a soft moisture that coats my tongue, that makes me want to eat all of her, until I am sated, stuffed. Between the soft folds of skin, I find the hardening peak of her clit, catch it softly between my teeth until I hear her release her breath, a sound that's audible even above the soft whine of the dogs.

Too soon, I feel her hands in my hair, those natural nails edging against my scalp, and then she's pulling me up, despite my protests, despite the way my knees don't want to unbend.

Her lips find mine again and suck the flavor from them, tongue glazing the corners of my mouth with a ragged growl.

"I want..." I start, but then her fingers are opening my jeans, one hand sliding inside them. Her skin is cool against my heat, her fingers hard against my softness. She twirls one, lets it find its way inside with a soft circle that sets all my nerves alight. I push into her touch, asking for more, deeper, but she pulls away. Thankfully, it's only to return a moment later. This time, two fingers dip and roll inside me, scraping me in the way that makes me want more, so much more. I push my hips into her hand—everything around us is gone, the room, the dog, even YoYo. I can't see any farther than her face, her eyes watching mine as she circles my clit with her thumb, her other fingers fucking me, beckoning along the swell of my g-spot, making me ache and buck and groan. Around and around her fingers, harder and harder until I'm dizzy from wanting and lack of air. And then the kissing, the tongue and lips that take away whatever small breath is left, that forces my head backward, her other hand curling tight at the back of my neck.

"Come for me," she says against my mouth, in that same shy voice that she had at the beginning. It's like a plea, a beg, the best kind of request, and when she flicks the nail of her thumb across my clit in unison, I can't help but obey.

I think I've come so hard my vision is fucked up, flickering on and off like someone else is blinking my eyelids for me. But then I realize it's actually the lights flickering overhead, and not my eyeballs. My breath is fast and quick and Marnie is smiling at me. She pulls her fingers from me, brings them to her face, and sucks them into her mouth. That image—her coated fingers slipping between her still-glossed lips—and suddenly I want all over again.

Another light flicker, and I turn just enough to see YoYo heading to the front door. Her free hand raises as she reaches the front door, making her signature O-symbol, only this time, a shiny quarter is caught in the circle of her fingers as she slips out the door, locking it behind her.

I turn back to Marnie. She's moved back a little, biting over her lower lip with her square white teeth, still watching me through her dark lashes. Her eyes aren't pleading, not anymore, but I want them to be again. I want to see them, looking up at me, dark and aching. I have a sudden desire to hear her beg and whine beneath me, to watch her breath catch in her throat before she howls, a sound of pleasure that can't be caught or captured. That image I had earlier—her bent over my couch, pushing her skirt up around her waist—is now reversed. I want her to be the one who bends me, who musses me up. I want her to fuck me, fingers, tongue, silicone, I don't care, I just want to feel her pushing herself to the depths of me, telling me to come again and again.

"So, about the dog..." she says, eyebrows up, licking her fingers clean between words.

"There's an easy way to make sure you're the right girl for Roxie," I say when my breath is back enough that I can speak.

"And that is?"

"Come home with me." I don't know if I'm more stunned by my offer or by the way my voice sounds—confident, sure, husked with want.

She flashes a soft smile, leans her hips into me again. I am all liquid from the waist down, melting, and I feel like if I move away from her, I might just slip to the ground. "What about the paperwork?"

"We can do that first thing in the morning," I say.

She leans in again and she kisses me, parting my lips with the point of her tongue to draw it along the front of my teeth. I suck her bottom lip into my mouth, taste the sweet strength of her and me mixing, until we're both moaning, muffled and gasping. Behind us, Roxie's tail thumps again as he settles his head on his paws, eyes closing.

"Take me home," Marnie says. For a moment, the words are caught and caged between us and then they are running free, and I'm tangling my fingers inside Marnie's, tugging her forward, leading the way. There are so many things I want to do to this woman, so many ways to open her, tease and please, to explore that steeled strength beneath her perfectly pretty exterior.

See, what'd I tell you? You can tell so much about how a woman fucks by the stray she decides to take home.

FARMHAND

Miel Rose

The road was a piece of shit and their driveway was worse. I had taken the left where the directions said and the driveway turned out to be another mile of bumpy ride worse than the near-constant washboard of the main road. My truck was old and the shocks were not what they used to be. I was grinding the enamel off my teeth and wondering if anyone could possibly live out here when I turned a bend and saw the homestead.

I had answered an ad I found in the paper. "Queer couple seeks farmhand to help out in exchange for rent. Must have prior experience with gardening and goats."

I found it in the personals section, which would have been weird, except for the fact that most of the women seeking women in this paper were looking for non-sexual relationships. I still looked every week, though, hoping for something along the lines of "high femme top seeks butch service bottom with strong tongue."

I was at some kind of crossroads any way you looked at it.

Between lovers, between jobs, couch surfing at a friend's. I had been looking for a way to get out of town, and this seemed like the golden ticket.

I called the number and spoke to Taylor, told her about growing up rural with big gardens and my experiences on some CSAs outside the city. We set up an interview for me to see the place.

Which was why I had driven down that crazy-ass dirt road. I got out of the truck to look around. The house was beautiful, one of those gorgeous old New England farmhouses you know is freezing in the winter. The yard was a jungle, tall grass mixed with flowers that had probably been an intentional garden once. I walked around the house and found an herb garden in better order, a chicken coop, vegetable gardens in various stages of cultivation, and the goat barn and pasture stretching out into the distance.

I was walking around the house, figuring I'd get to some kind of door eventually, when I heard the noises coming from a window in front of me. Blood rushed to my cheeks. I thought, *it would have to be some kind of antique bed frame to make that kind of racket.* As I neared the window the sounds became distinct, the squeak of springs, whimpers, groans, and the slap of skin hitting skin.

I kept walking like I was on autopilot. I don't know what I was thinking. I don't make a habit of spying on people through their windows, I swear. I kept walking, barely breathing, and peeked through the window past the white curtains.

The bed was in the corner of the room across from the window. On the bed was a beautiful naked woman on her knees, her hands gripping the old, squeaky frame. My eyes were drawn to her large breasts, shaking from the fucking she was getting. She had long brown hair, messy and tangled, and a luscious body that quivered and shook as the square hands on her hips pulled her into each thrust.

I ripped my eyes away from her body to get a look at her partner. This was Taylor, I guessed. She was really handsome, and definitely butch. I had a brief moment feeling the strangeness of reading someone's gender while watching them naked and fucking. I had the feeling that I would recognize this person's gender blindfolded. It wasn't her short, dark hair, or the fact that she was wearing the cock, fucking this beautiful woman from behind so hard you could hear their bodies slapping together. It was one of those things about gender that you can't put your finger on, no matter how much you theorize and debate. It's something you know in your gut. I watched her lean over her lover's back and sink her teeth into the flesh of her shoulder. The luscious woman, Lilly, I guessed, screamed and arched her back, grinding her ass back at Taylor. Taylor reached around Lilly's body, found her clit, and rubbed at it, making her convulse.

That broke the spell. I pulled my eyes away and continued around the house.

I sat down in the back of my truck, took a deep breath, and counted to one hundred. They might still be in bed, but our appointment was for half an hour ago, so I went to their front door and knocked real loud. I felt shaky and nervous, not to mention horny as hell. My briefs were sticking to my crotch in a not-so-comfortable way. I was still blushing when Taylor opened the front door.

She had put on jeans and a T-shirt. Her breasts were bound under her shirt and I realized that I didn't know if Taylor iden-tified as a woman. I was feeling really disoriented and tried desperately to get my mental footing.

"Hey, you must be Jess! Come on in, we're running late this morning." I tried to smile as I let myself be ushered into the house. "I'm Taylor, by the way." She held out her hand and I shook it, remembering her fingers rubbing Lilly's pussy moments earlier. I wondered if she had bothered to wash her hands.

"Beautiful place you got here," I said, looking around and trying to feel less awkward.

"Oh, thanks. I inherited it from my grandma when she passed. Me and Lilly have done a lot of work on it," she looked around as she said this, beaming with pride. She led me into the kitchen and opened the refrigerator. "Lilly's getting dressed. We were thinking we could make some lunch, then give you the major tour."

"That sounds great," I said just as Lilly skipped in.

She had braided her hair into two messy braids, which she flung over her shoulders as she came in. She walked in smiling radiantly, beaming at me in the most disarming way. My knees got weak as I watched her walk toward me, her body as sexy clothed as it had been laid out naked on the bed. She bounced as she walked, making her hips and breasts shake. I could tell she felt good inside her body, and it made me want to feel good inside her body too.

"Hi! You must be Jess! I'm Lilly." She extended a slim, calloused hand. "Welcome. Did Taylor tell you that we're both starving and need to make some food? Are you hungry?"

We were standing in a close triangle and I was reeling from their energy, the heat and smells radiating from their bodies.

"Baby, I think we're overwhelming Jess. Hey, if you don't mind me asking, what pronoun do you prefer?" As Taylor asked this, Lilly was reaching above my head for a colander and I got a good view of the tops of her breasts pushing out over the bra she was wearing under her tank top.

"Um, oh, yeah, I use female pronouns," I stammered. "And you?"

"Same, female. I used to identify more as male when I was younger, but I'm finding that shifts as I age. I identify more as a butch dyke now, as unpopular as that is these days."

This made Lilly giggle, and Taylor grabbed her and kissed her neck. "And Miss Femme Princess here also uses female pronouns, but she can tell you how she IDs herself."

Lilly wiggled out of Taylor's arms, muttering, "Femme princess, my ass," and then louder, "I'm going to get some greens for salad." She strode out the door and I watched her ass sway from side to side before I realized I was staring. I looked at Taylor, hoping she hadn't caught me looking, and saw her watching Lilly too, absorbed in her own appreciation.

She shook her head and turned to me, smiling, and said, "Let's go get the eggs. I promised Lilly I'd make soufflé."

Living with Lilly and Taylor was awkward. I felt intimidated by their confidence, the sense of belonging they both exuded. They had some basic contentment going on that should have been a birthright, but most people I knew had missed it.

Then there was the fact that I seemed to get hard every time I was in the same room with either one of them. I thought this would pass as I got used to their company, but if anything it got worse.

At night, I could hear their sex from my room. I would create pictures in my head to match the noises coming from their bedroom. Lilly did not take it quietly. I would rub my clit fast and furious, thinking of Taylor fucking her or eating her pussy while they moaned and banged away on that old squeaky bed frame. I imagined myself in Taylor's place, laid out on top of Lilly's delicious body, fucking her deep with my cock. Sometimes, though I shied away from the thought during daylight hours, I would imagine myself in Lilly's position, getting plowed viciously by

Taylor, getting fucked so hard my teeth rattled. Five seconds of these thoughts and I was screaming my come into my pillow.

I had always been attracted to femmes, especially tough-ass femmes who could beat the shit out of me if they wanted, or would if I asked nicely. It was something familiar, something I knew. I had never been comfortable with my attraction to other butches, though, never felt safe around it. I would occasionally have drunken sex with a buddy, but considered myself lucky if we could meet each other's eyes the next morning.

It complicated things that I grew to look up to Taylor so much. It's a funny thing not knowing if you want to be someone or fuck them, and knowing you definitely want to fuck their wife. By no means did I have it figured out by the time I started sleeping with them.

It happened with Lilly first.

She and Taylor had planned a trip into town. Lilly came into the kitchen that morning decked out in this sexy little gingham sundress, high-heeled sandals, and full makeup. She didn't go into town that often, and though she definitely presented femme around the farm, I had never seen her dress up like that before. I admit I blushed and looked away real quick. When they left, Lilly kissed me on the cheek, leaving a trace of her lipstick, and told me to be good.

I spent the morning doing my chores, stretching out the tension building in my body. I was constantly aware of how hard I was, and by lunchtime I was throbbing.

After eating I went into my room and took out my harness, my biggest cock, and my favorite porno. As much as I liked living with Lilly and Taylor, keeping my libido in check was starting to get strenuous.

I went into the living room and popped the porno into the

VCR. It was an indie production I'd bought on sale and I liked it because the women had bigger, realistic bodies, and they seemed to enjoy getting fucked more than in other porn I've seen.

The movie opened with this beautiful woman, a voluptuous brunette, sitting at her desk typing. She was a secretary and was about to be seduced and fucked by her boss. It was clichéd, sure, but it's the kind of shit that gets me off every time.

I reached under my cock and got as much cunt juice on my hand as possible. I ran my hand down my cock, and the wet slickness against the give of the silicone made the hair stand up on my arms. The beautiful girl on the screen knelt down and took her boss's dick all the way into her mouth, her eyes bulging as her lips stretched around the base.

I closed my eyes and imagined Lilly kneeling in front of me, taking my cock between her red lips. My hand moved faster on my dick and I slid my other hand around, slipping two fingers up my cunt.

I opened my eyes and the brunette was still blowing her boss. He had taken her tits out of her blouse and was playing with them as she sucked him. He squeezed her nipples and she moaned loud around his cock. I closed my eyes again and thought of Lilly's gorgeous tits. I remembered the first time I saw her, Taylor fucking her so hard from behind that her tits bounced up and slapped down against her torso. I groaned and moved my fingers faster in and out of my cunt.

Then, above the TV sex noises, I heard the screen door bang shut and the click of heels on wood floor.

My eyes flew open and there she was in all her gingham sundressed glory, standing in the doorway with her hand on her beautiful hip. It happened that fast.

"I told you to be good," she said, tilting her head and looking me up and down. Then she looked over at the TV screen where the brunette was straddling the now-seated boss's lap and bouncing up and down on his cock. "Nice," Lilly said, and walked toward me.

"Hey, Lilly, I'm really sorry you found me like this," I stammered as I tried to collect myself and stand up.

"Yeah, I bet you're sorry," she said and pushed me back down on the couch.

She was right where I'd imagined her minutes earlier, on her knees in front of my cock.

"My, what a big boy you are," she purred. She looked me right in the eye, raised her hand level with the head of my cock, and flicked it. She actually flicked it. Then she said, "You think you can work this monster?"

This challenge made my clit rock hard under my cock. This woman was my wettest dream. She was also married, for all intents and purposes, so what was she doing between my legs, smirking at my cock?

"Lilly? What's going on? What about—" She shushed me, crawled up my body, and wrapped her fingers around my throat.

"I know you want me," she said, squirming in a way that made my body feel like it was dissolving into the couch. "I see how you watch me." She nuzzled her face into my neck and licked her wicked tongue across my jugular vein. "I bet you think about me when you touch yourself."

"Ohh, fuck, Lilly, what are you doing to me?"

"Exactly what you want me to do, sugar," she said, and kissed me full on the mouth, slipping her tongue between my lips. She tasted so good I groaned into her mouth.

Breaking the kiss, she said, "Hands behind your head, now." It was an abrupt order, but I complied with speed. "Good boy," she said, leaning forward to run her tongue over my bottom lip.

"Fuck," she said, standing up, "I'm so fucking wet." She

slipped her panties down her legs and threw them into the corner. Pulling her dress up around her waist, she said, "See what you did to me, Jess?"

Her pussy hair was trimmed short and her clit was so swollen it stuck straight out between her puffy cunt lips. I wanted her so bad.

"Oh, god, I want to taste you. Let me suck you, Lilly, please? Let me touch you. I'll do anything, please."

"Maybe next time. Take off your cock."

"What?"

"Boy, I know you heard me," she said in her no-nonsense voice.

Wondering what she was after, I brought my hands to the buckle of my harness.

"Hand it to me," she said and, trembling inside, I did.

She stepped into the leg straps and adjusted the harness to fit her luscious body. Call me dense, but that was when it hit me that she intended to fuck me with my own cock. My cunt got wetter than it'd been in years.

"Mmm, it feels good to wear a cock again," she said, jutting her hips forward and starring down at it. "Now, lie down on the couch and spread your legs for me."

I did as she said. I wanted to be good for her, to please her however I could, and to be honest, I desperately wanted that cock inside me.

She crawled onto the couch between my legs and spread them farther apart. She ran her thumb up my slit, moaned, and put the cock head at the mouth of my cunt.

She pushed into me and leaned forward to kiss me. I felt a fullness expand inside me that got bigger as she started to fuck me.

Her teeth sank into my bottom lip. She moaned into my mouth and fucked me harder. She was as loud fucking as she was getting fucked and her noises were all *girl*, a constant reminder that this was a femme fucking me.

As I got closer she got louder, saying, "Come on, sweet boy, come for me. Come for me before I come up inside you." She rotated her hips, twisting the cock inside me, and I went off like fucking dynamite, coming hard around the thick base of her cock.

Things got weird after that. I could tell she wanted to talk, but I panicked and ran, hid out in my room for the rest of the day, playing music loud, pretending I couldn't hear her knocking. I heard Taylor drive up around dark and wondered where the hell she'd been, and why Lilly had come home early without her.

I skulked into the kitchen the next day and Taylor was waiting for me.

"Grab your sleeping bag, I want to take you someplace," she said, and lugged a couple of heavy-looking bags out to her truck.

I have to admit I was scared shitless, but Taylor had always been kind to me and a part of me trusted her more than I should have, knowing her such a short time. I followed her out to the truck and we rode in excruciating silence for thirty-five miles.

The hike was short, the bags were heavy, and we were sweating like pigs by the time we reached the spot she was looking for.

"This land belongs to my uncle, but he never comes here anymore." It was the first thing she'd said since the kitchen. Then, just like that, she launched into it: "Lilly feels real bad about yesterday. She should have just come out and told you that we'd talked about you two having sex, that I'm okay with it. Our relationship is pretty defined and she doesn't get to express top energy very often. I think she got a little carried away."

My mouth hung open, I know it did. Whatever I had been expecting, this wasn't it.

"So," Taylor continued, "in an effort not to repeat her mistake, I'd like to make it known that we've also discussed how much I'd like to fuck you. If you're not interested, it's cool. We can still sit down and negotiate something between you and Lilly. I know it could get messy, but I'm willing to give it a try, see if it works."

Taylor looked down at her hands while she talked, and it occurred to me that even a confident person fears rejection. I could find no way past the lump in my throat to speak, so I simply reached for her hand and drew her toward me.

Her eyes locked on mine and she said, "Are you sure?"

I swallowed, cleared my throat, and said, "I'm sure."

Then her mouth was on mine. Taylor slid her tongue into my mouth, then sucked my tongue into hers. She broke the kiss to arrange the pile of sleeping bags on the ground and pushed me back onto them. Climbing on top of me, she wedged her thigh hard between my legs and continued the kiss, sucking my bottom lip, sliding down to my neck, sinking her teeth into me.

"You are so fucking hot, Jess." Her hands found my hard nipples and she pinched them, twisting. "Why don't you take your shirt off for me."

I wriggled out of my T-shirt, exposing my chest to her. The heat and wet of her mouth on my tit made me crazy. She devoured me, sucking as much of my flesh into her mouth as would fit. I thrust my hips against her thigh and her hand snaked down to my crotch, cupping me over my jeans. She unzipped my pants and I helped her pull them down along with my underwear.

She grinned at me, reached into her back pocket, and pulled out a glove. "Always be prepared," she said. Her gloved hand found my cunt wet and swollen. She plunged into me and I yelped, surprised at how sore I was.

Taylor pulled out gently and I said, embarrassed, "Sorry, I guess I'm a little sore from yesterday. It's been a while..."

She grinned at me. "Yeah, Lilly said that was a monster you were strapping." Her fingers pressed against my perineum and slid past to my asshole. "How about this?" she asked as she circled my hole with her fingers.

"Ohhh, god," I said, and rocked my hips into her.

She reached into the nearest pack and pulled out a bottle of lube, squirted some onto her glove. It must be some kind of natural law that lube is always cold at first, even on hot days. I felt my ass clench around the tip of her finger at the shock of it. Her teeth locked around my nipple and a noise I didn't recognize as my own escaped my throat. She slid another finger up inside me and started fucking me with short, hard thrusts, her fingers pushed in as far as they could go. Her hand hit my perineum with each stroke, sending dull hammer blows of pleasure along my nerves.

I got lost in the conflict of feeling, her sharp wolf teeth chewing my nipples, the dull thud of her fingers fucking me, the fullness in my ass as she slid a third finger inside me. Every sensation seemed to be set on overwhelming me with its intensity, till I never wanted it to end and simultaneously prayed to come, fearing I might burst some organ with all that pressure building inside.

She looked me in the eye and said, "Why don't you rub that clit for me, it looks ready to explode."

My hand flew to my clit and started stroking with a hard, vicious intensity. I watched Taylor's face as she watched me rub my cunt, and that alone could have pushed me over. But I also had her fingers pounding my asshole, her other hand putting increasing pressure on my windpipe, her filthy whispers in my ear telling me to come.

And I did, with those earthquake spasms that orgasms are made of when you have fingers buried deep in your ass. I shook so hard she had to hold me down in case I flopped away from her.

It has never stopped being strange to me, that space after you come, after the beast of lust falls asleep and you are lying there with another person who has just watched you double over in orgasmic spasms, shrieking like a maniac. Someone who has played an instrumental role in your orgasm, seen you vulnerable outside of your shell, felt your slick and swollen internals.

I expected the worst; it's a bad habit, but easy to pick up in this world.

Taylor was a master at making me comfortable, though. It's a crazy shock to see tenderness where you look for disgust. It's a shock to find yourself fifteen minutes later, still naked, wrestling the fully clothed person who just fucked your ass. To be so engrossed telling your life story to this person, so caught up in the feeling of their arms around you, you don't even realize that it's getting late until the beauty of the sunset registers in your brain.

We collected our things and I thought about what I'd been up to in the last two days. Where would this bring me, fucking my housemates and semi-employers? I wondered what it would be like walking into the house and seeing Lilly, knowing she knew what I'd been doing with her lover all day. I wondered how I would feel going to bed alone knowing they would have each other, like always. I wondered where and how I could fit into this equation, and if it would prove too difficult for someone like me who only took freshman algebra.

I wondered and worried a lot on our way back, and I came to a place for the first time in my life where making the decision to stop worrying seemed like a possibility. I had always been a chronic borrower of trouble, and it had kept me out of a whole lot of bad situations—but a lot of good ones too.

Sitting in Taylor's truck on the drive home, I made the decision to take things as they came. And if Lilly and Taylor got sick of me, kicked me out, broke my heart, well, as my grandpa used to say, I would burn that bridge when I came to it.

A DATE WITH
SHARON TATE

Valerie Alexander

My best friend and I planned the Dead Movie Star Party mostly because we were bored, but also because she wanted an excuse to dress up like Humphrey Bogart. We were also sticking to a resolution to throw more parties instead of complaining about the lack thereof, and I had a vintage suit that made me look, I was convinced, like Cary Grant in *His Girl Friday*. It was also a creative way to take my mind off being dumped by my girlfriend, Shandra, for an offensively bland little femme with big hair.

Jules, my best friend, knew enough not to ask if Shandra would attend. Jules knew enough not to bring it up at all. Some people like to endlessly hash out what went wrong, lament their mistakes. I don't. I am private and I am methodical, and I preferred to direct my energies into a detailed strategy for getting Shandra back. That strategy was still under construction, but I had spent the summer so far building an elaborate tree house in my backyard, retiling the bathroom, and trying not to drink as much as I had the last time I cheated on and lost a woman. The Dead Movie Star Party was the latest distraction from my anguished, howling libido.

"I'm impressed with how many responses we've gotten," Jules said, looking over her spreadsheet. "So far over sixty people have RSVPed and we only have eight celebrity repeats."

I looked over her shoulder. "Who?"

Marilyn Monroe was no surprise and neither was James Dean, but Elvis was. "I don't even know if we should allow him," Jules ruminated. "He's really more of a musician…"

"He made tons of movies, he counts. But he's the only musician who gets in; I don't want to see one Janis Joplin or Kurt Cobain."

Jules looked embarrassed. "I already told Kim from the skate shop that she could come as John Lennon."

"No! Call her back and say no. You need to be more firm, Jules."

We were aiming for a silver-screen, slightly morbid ambience. The kind of party where butches could revel in their old-school suaveness and femmes could vamp as high as they wanted. I'd always loved Halloween, but in recent years it seemed to have morphed into some kind of trashy Frederick's of Hollywood cliché. So Jules and I decided everyone needed an additional costume party to bring back the elegance and effort of a good impersonation. The boys hadn't been hard to convince at all, of course, but we were surprised by how enthusiastic the dykes had been.

"Oh good, Hilary is coming as Marlon Brando," she said. "And Shannon is going to be—uh-oh—Judy Garland."

"It's okay. We can have male and female Judys."

"And Sophie is going to be Rita Hayworth. I can see that. Are you still going as Cary Grant?"

"Of course."

Whether I facially resembled Cary Grant was debatable, but he was the most natural actor for me to mimic. I had his height and broad shoulders, and his short dark hair, and I liked to think I had his courtly elegance—when I made the effort. It was less definite who my ex-girlfriend Shandra would impersonate, if she attended. She actually had a very conventional, actressy prettiness, from her long cool body to her high cheekbones and dazzling smile. Yet it was for that reason she lacked distinction. Being blonde, she was told by strangers that she looked like every actress under the rainbow. I thought she looked like Sharon Tate, the actress murdered by the Manson family, and liked calling her Shandra Tate. But she bristled when I said it, as if I were intimating a violent and premature end for her.

"Don't say that, say anyone but her," she'd say, twisting her rings.

"But she was beautiful, and you do look like her. Why does it matter how she died? If she had lived more recently, you'd hear it all the time. It's a compliment, baby."

Shandra's looks had brought her little benefit in the world. When I met her, she was the intimidated girlfriend of an obnoxious power dyke I'd never been able to stand. Shandra worked in the university library, and as a grad student, I began visiting it on a regular basis to flirt with her. She seemed shy, her big hazel eyes fluttering down with an uncertainty I'd find annoyingly passive in any other woman. Somehow with her, it jerked at my heart. I could tell she liked me, and so it was with half-bravado, half-foolishness that I pushed up her skirt and seduced her one day in the special collections room.

She was standing on a little stool, hunting through a filing cabinet. She looked, in her tight sweater and pencil skirt, like a dirty librarian ripe for the plundering. Her little grunt of satisfaction when she found the right file just undid me, and I pushed up her skirt with both hands. She stopped moving. "Oh, come on," she said, but she didn't protest further. I touched the back of her knees, ran my fingertips down the tensed muscles of her thighs. Her panties were at my face level and I wanted to tongue her through the nylon. Instead I pulled them down to her knees to make her feel more vulnerable. Shandra sucked in her breath. I touched her clit, making her jump with surprise, and forced her legs open a bit. Then I unleashed my tongue on her like a robber baron, stealing both her heart and her pussy for about twelve seconds before a sense of loyalty to her girlfriend kicked in. *I can't,* she said. I stopped and asked her to dinner. She said yes, and before our appetizers came, she was mine.

Later I learned that her girlfriend had been quite the bastard, belittling Shandra in public and insulting her taste in everything from clothes to music. My view of myself changed from a poacher to a liberator. "I will never do less than cherish you the way you deserve," I told her, pinning her against the wall to bite her throat, "and you deserve the best."

I was always a very generous top in bed, but with her I pulled out stops I didn't know I had. Perhaps because her ex was butch too and that made me competitive, perhaps because I didn't know how to emotionally cater to someone I loved that much, I overwhelmed her with sex in the hopes she'd never leave. I saturated her with sex, fucked her until our skin seemed welded together, made her come over and over and over with my hands, my tongue, my harem of cocks. I taught her that she could come from having her nipples bitten, I introduced her to the wondrous potentials of her ass, I adored her and fed her by hand before bathing her and fucking her into a hot sweaty mess all over again. I told her every day how beautiful and rare she was. And she was mine, permanently I felt, until the night I stupidly and drunkenly went home from a bar with someone else.

I never knew how many people were jealous of our relationship until I counted all the gossip bunnies who rang her up and told her before I even got home.

Over the coming weeks, the Dead Movie Star Party crystallized into the event of the summer. Maybe it was because Jules and I picked a night when nothing else was going on, but people we hadn't even invited were coming, lost friends and ex-lovers and rivals and homebodies who never went out. I became tyrannical in my insistence that no one would be admitted without a costume. "Dress up as Lassie, Bela Lugosi—I don't care—but you had better be a deceased actor." I felt sure this would cut down on attendees, since we were already past house capacity and quickly filling the backyard.

"We have to make sure Gillian doesn't come," I said to Jules a week before the party. Gillian was the woman I'd cheated on Shandra with.

Jules threw me a skeptical look. "Why? It's not like Shandra is going to be here."

"I know, but just in case."

Jules took off her glasses and polished them. "She wouldn't set foot in here. Remember how she said she never would have dated you if she'd known what a bad reputation you had? "

"I don't see why that matters. She did date me. She knows all those other mistakes were from when I was young. She knows I've changed."

"My point is, she took a chance on you and you blew it."

That was logical, but it wasn't accurate. It was true that I had had a bit of a reputation when we met—nothing horrible, just a few girls with their feelings hurt, another cheating incident— but Shandra had had over a year to learn that I was no longer that selfish or cavalier. It was just her pride over my drunken mistake with Gillian keeping us apart, because what Jules didn't know was that Shandra still wanted me.

I'd seen her three weeks ago at a Thai café, eating dinner with her new girlfriend. I was picking up take-out. We saw each other at the same time, though her girlfriend didn't see me. She loftily ignored my wave. Okay, then. I brazenly studied the new girlfriend. Femme, tiny, not Shandra's type. Nothing that could be a real replacement for me. As soon as my order arrived, Shandra rose and headed for the restroom. I left the bag on the counter and followed her in. She couldn't meet my eyes: we both knew she had wanted me to come after her. I backed her against the wall.

"You're so arrogant," she said.

"If that's how you see it," I replied. I cupped her pussy and she arched her back, pressing against my hand with that little grunt for about five heartbeats.

Then she erupted into indignation and said, "You know I'm with April!" and flounced out. Shades of the day we met. But this time I let her go.

Since then an acidic jealousy haunted me in sporadic bursts. I couldn't sleep at night thinking of them in each other's arms. I couldn't even imagine that little bitch fucking my girlfriend with anything like the power and passion I had, so I told myself she wasn't a threat. But the thought of their breath on each other's cheek made me crazy; made me remember the way Shandra's head had migrated to my pillow each night, her breasts snug against my back, the soft trip of her fingers over my stomach. It all made me want to punch something.

The party filled up faster than we thought possible. My friend Crystal, dressed as River Phoenix, worked the door to make sure only people in costume got in. It was a mercifully cool night but the house got hot and we kept the AC on high, constantly restocking the bottles of beer on ice. As the backyard filled up, I was called on more and more to show off the new tree house I had built. I was proud of this tree house. It wrapped around my big oak tree and had a lookout deck with a view of my neighbor's garden. It had sleeping quarters as well.

"I wish I could build," said a guy who'd come as Jayne Mansfield. "You're so talented!"

"Anyone can do this if they take the time to learn," I said. I actually didn't believe that, but I liked to sound modest.

Then I saw her. Sharon Tate was standing in my backyard in a white sequined minidress, hands twisting together as she looked around. Long ironed platinum hair, '60s makeup, angelic and cool: Shandra had knocked it out of the park. I leaned over the tree house railing with a grin as I watched her searching for me. Yes, her stupid placebo of a girlfriend was with her. I mentally erased her presence as I drank in the anxious need in Shandra's eyes. She wanted to find me, wanted me to see how she'd dressed up for me. I knew what it meant.

Most of the other guests were glancing at her without recognition. Even if they knew who Sharon Tate was, there was no seminal outfit or trait to signify it. At last one of the older queens wandered by and gasped, "Oh my god, *Valley of the Dolls*! You look *perfect*!" Thank god someone here knew their Hollywood history. A good host would have climbed down and greeted her and the girlfriend, but instead I just savored her visual splendor until she looked up and saw me. She scowled.

I climbed down the ladder in my suit, hoping it didn't look as undignified as it felt. "Ladies," I said in my best Cary Grant voice. The little girlfriend gave me a disgusted look. That's right, eat your heart out, I said to her silently. You'll be going home alone tonight in your half-assed Audrey Hepburn costume.

"This is great," Shandra said. "Everyone actually dressed up, I can't believe it."

I can't believe you came was the natural response, but I was mostly interested in getting her alone. "Can I get you two something to drink? Shandra, your vodka and tonic?"

As expected, the fake girlfriend bristled and said, "*I'll* get it for her," and disappeared. Too easy.

"Yes, everyone really looks great," Shandra repeated. She was nervous. She tucked a long strand of hair behind her ear, glanced at me, then looked away.

I wanted to tell her how beautiful she was, that just looking at her squeezed my heart and flooded my briefs. That dressing up for me was the ultimate gift, flag of surrender and erotic proposal all in one, and that I was going to worship and honor her for as long as she would tolerate me. But she wasn't quite ready for that. I saw it in her tense bare shoulders, her guarded eyes.

"We've been planning it for weeks, me and Jules," I said. "I've been working night and day to finish tiling the bathroom in time."

"Oh, you retiled your bathroom?" We could have been strangers, the way we were talking. "What colors?"

"Black, white, and sea-green. Do you want to take a look?"

We were ever so proper as we walked into the house, me making sure to give a wide berth to the makeshift bar where the fake girlfriend was getting Shandra's drink. I permitted myself one hand on the small of her back to guide her into the bathroom and then shut the door. As soon as it clicked shut, raw lust washed over me. We were alone in a room at last.

"It looks great," Shandra said. As if perceiving my change in mood, she backed against the counter. Her minidress was riding really high on her legs, high enough that I could lift it just an inch or two and see her underwear.

I looked up and realized she had caught me looking at her crotch. "Nice dress."

I walked over until I towered over her. Shandra had always liked how tall I was, and she bit her lip now and looked up coquettishly as if waiting to be kissed. I didn't touch her. Instead I leaned in close to her and said, "I built a tree house too. You should come out and see it."

She frowned. I had made a tactical error by using my sex voice. "Don't hit on me. You know I'm here with April."

"Fuck April," I said. "Just go on one date with me. We'll start over. You can have all the time you need to trust me again."

Shandra made a scoffing noise. "I'm a married woman now."

I laughed. I couldn't help it, it was such an obvious exaggeration intended to hurt me. Now Shandra looked furious, her face going red under the makeup. I'd forgotten how gorgeous she was when she was mad. She started to leave and I took her arm to stop her.

"Don't manhandle me," she said.

I released her arm. She didn't move and I leaned my leg against hers. She looked at the sink, looked at the new tiles. Then she looked at me.

My mouth was on hers in less than a second, recapturing all the heat and sweetness of her tongue. She kissed me back just as passionately and I leaned in to pin her against the counter. I wanted to smell and taste every part of her, but her tight vintage dress had her pretty much imprisoned as my hands stroked her breasts and legs. "One date," I said in her ear, "one date, your terms," because I wanted her to agree to a meeting beyond this momentary lapse in sanity. I lifted her up and sat her on the black granite countertop and she leaned back and opened her legs for me. Oh my god. She was wearing a thong, just a little scrap of white fabric, and before I could even go near it, she slid it down herself, spread her thighs, and looked at me. She wanted me to fuck her. The sex between her and that stupid girlfriend was as boring as I'd guessed, and she needed me to fuck her hard and good, just like I used to.

But I didn't. "One date," I said. I didn't let myself look at her pussy. "A date where we sit down and talk. Just go on an actual date with me, Shandra."

She reached between her legs and stroked her clit. "Fuck me," she whispered.

"No." She looked surprised and hurt and I would have done almost anything to bring back that earlier look of pure lust. Instead I said: "I don't fuck married women anymore. Break up with her, go on a date with me, and give me one more chance."

Someone tried to come in and pounded on the door. "How long you guys gonna be?" they yelled.

Shandra jumped down from the counter, pulling up her thong and adjusting her dress with a tight mouth. She was embarrassed. "Shandra," I said, but she walked out and left me standing there as miserable as I'd ever been in my life.

I let a Natalie Wood into the bathroom and walked slowly into the backyard. If this was all I was to her now, the butch ex who was good in bed and worthless out of it, then I was done with her. To my disgust, I was shaking. I got a beer, ignored everyone calling to me and went back up the tree house ladder. Thank god it was empty. I walked onto the lookout deck and stared at my neighbor's garden.

The tap of high heels sounded on the ladder. Another drag queen, no doubt. I chugged my beer, put on my game face, and turned around. And there she was, Sharon Tate carefully climbing into the tree house, the sequins of her dress softly clicking against the wood. She hesitated on the highest rung and gave me an uncertain smile. I helped her in like a gentleman and she staggered a little on her heels anyhow. I steadied her but didn't try to hold on to her.

She adjusted her hair. "One date," she said.

I hung back, though my every cell wanted to embrace her. "Oh, I don't know. I wouldn't want to date a married woman."

She gave me a loaded look. "So divorce me."

Without taking her eyes from me, she reached behind her and unzipped that ridiculously tight dress. I watched in fascination as she casually pulled it over her head, so easily, despite the way it had confounded me in the bathroom. Then she unhooked the tiny lace bra she was wearing and dropped it. Her breasts swayed as she walked toward me in just the thong and the heels. I could barely breathe.

"This doesn't count as the date, just to get that clear," I said.

She smiled and ran her fingers through my hair. "Enough," she said and kissed my earlobe. "You'll get your date. Though I do like you needy and anxious."

Her fingers slid down and stroked my mouth. Her touch almost undid me just like it always had, evoking memories of her softness and her fierceness, her small breasts and her heart-shaped ass. I closed my eyes, wanting to drown in the smell and feel of her for a moment. She took my hand and placed it on her pussy. Somehow her thong had come down as well and I groaned at the feel of her bare folds.

She leaned back against the tree house railing, spreading her legs and moving my fingers on her clit. I watched, mesmerized, as if we were playing a duet on her skin. Shandra naked in high heels had always been one of my all-time great sexual visuals, and I stepped back to take it all in. Then I knelt down and paid homage to her pussy, licking her and sucking her until she opened her legs so wide her thigh muscles visibly strained. The faint briny taste of her was so painfully sweet that tears almost pricked my eyes. Shandra squirmed shamelessly against my face, smearing her juices over my cheeks, my chin. She'd always been uninhibited about getting her pussy serviced; it was one of the things I loved about her. But we had other territory to cover.

I stood up and roughly pushed her around so she was facing my neighbor's garden. Then I bent her over the railing until her ass stuck out at an obscene angle, as if inviting any passing stranger to ravish her. I undid my pants and took out my cock, which I'd worn just for her. I took the crown in my hand and rubbed it around her pussy, making her whimper. I eased it in just a bit, then paused until she tried to back up onto it. Oh, no. She wasn't going to get satisfied so easily. I smacked her bottom for such impudence, then pulled out. She leaned further over the railing until her ass was practically begging to be fucked. I teased her with just a finger, making her wiggle desperately. Then I positioned my cock again and drove all the way into her, deep and smooth, until she gasped.

"Fuck me," she begged, rocking her hips. She didn't care who heard us or saw us, she was pure unbridled desperation. I held her fast and fucked her hard, pushing her further and further into abandon until her tits and ass were bouncing in time with my thrusts. She rubbed her clit with a rhythm I remembered well, and then she was coming all over my cock as I watched her pussy contract. Slowly, slowly, I pulled out, while stroking her hips and her lower back.

She leaned against the railing for a bit, breathing hard. A fine sheen of sweat was drying on her spine and her long hair was a wild mess. When she turned around, I could see the heavy '60s eyeliner had smeared around her hazel eyes. She looked like a beautiful, fucked-out slut.

Without my saying a word, she knelt in front of me and sucked my cock clean. Looking up at me, she worked two fingers, then three into my pussy and rubbed me just the way I liked. I came in less than a minute in hot, glorious throbs that rocked my whole body. Shandra licked me clean and got to her feet, unsteady in her high heels.

It was like the world had gone away for those moments. Now it returned, the music of the party, the wind in the trees, the clink of beer bottles being fished from the cooler. I handed my naked movie star her dress and her underwear and watched her get dressed, and then we went back down to the party, perfect again.

BIENVENIDO

Anna Watson

B ack when I thought the closest I was ever going to get to pussy was taking deep breaths in the ladies' room at the mall, I sat boo-hooing on Shawna's bed, watching her model her cheerleader outfit. The year 2002 had been good to her; she'd been winning pageant after pageant and had become quite the drag queen around Dallas. As for me, I was complaining about dicks, as usual.

"The customer reviews said this one was really realistic," I whined. Realistic it might have been—for a seven-foot Martian with silly putty skin. Not so good for a 5'4" towheaded baby butch weighing in at 112, and that's with my Ropers on.

Can I tell you how badly I wanted a dick? My jeans felt empty and my heart beat lonely without one. So far, I'd broken the law and emptied my wallet three times sending out of state for "toys," and three times I had been bitterly disappointed.

"Oh, say, that reminds me." Shawna tore herself away from her reflection and beamed her big blue heartbreakers at me. She looked concerned. For me! I loved her dearly in that moment, for what can be more sustaining than the fierce, inconsistent love of a fabulously witty, self-absorbed, narcissistic drag queen?

I stopped fussing and waited, ready to hang on her every word. If I wasn't careful, she would go back to her pom-poms and leave me in the dark.

"Hmm, let's see, I met someone a couple of nights ago..."

Ah. Another conquest. But no, Shawna actually came over to me and perched her willowy body on my knees, playing with my hair. She was killing me.

"I've been worried about you, sugar." Shawna never calls me by my given name, which is Daisy. "You're dragging around and you just don't have the equipment you need." She'd been listening! I was grateful, since much of the time she treats me like so much background noise. Then I couldn't help looking down to where Shawna had her own equipment well tucked. She smacked me lightly and put a long finger under my chin to lift my head back up. "And, darlin', you so terribly need to get laid!" I jiggled her on my knees, frowning. This was an extremely sore spot, since, apart from a few awkward kisses with Brittany Dennison the summer of tenth grade, I was still a virgin six years later. Not that I hadn't tried, but no such luck, cowboy. Shawna leapt daintily to her feet. "Look, baby," she said, her attention already drifting back to the captivating image in the mirror. "You need to meet this fellow, Wade. Now where did I put that?"

Moments later, I was looking at a business card she'd dug out from the clutter on her dining room table. *I can make you a man* it said in curlicue print, then the name "Wade" and a local phone number.

"What's this?" I asked. "Isn't this a line from *The Rocky Horror Picture Show*?"

Shawna drew in her breath, visibly holding herself back from singing the entire soundtrack. "No," she said firmly. "It's what you need."

Back home, preparing my lonely bachelor's meal of frozen enchiladas, I stuck the card up on the fridge with my "Jesus loves you, but I'm his favorite" magnet, and a month later it was still there. By now, it was summer, classes at UT were over, and I was working a lot of hours at the caf and trying to make the nightclub scene whenever I could. I wasn't very good at it, though, too shy, too much of a lightweight when it came to substance abuse. And I knew I didn't look right. I was back to my tried-not-so-true method of going it with a sock stuffer and feeling more miserable by the day as my attempts to attract a girlfriend continued to fail. Shawna, after another spectacular first-place win complete with tears and tiara, had been incommunicado for several weeks, enjoying her celebrity status with an ever-changing lineup of suave suitors, but one evening she dropped by the duplex I rented with a bunch of roommates. She saw the card on the fridge as she searched without success for some chardonnay, surmised correctly that I'd never gotten around to making that call, snatched up the phone, dialed, and had me an appointment for the next day. She absolutely refused to go with me.

"This is something you have to do by yourself, young man," she told me before rushing off to her next engagement. "It will put hair on your chest."

That first time, Wade and I met at a Big Boy. It was about as unthreatening as pudding, but that didn't stop me from practically collapsing in a fit of nerves as I tried to get through the door. I was only there because Shawna had put it to me this way: If I canceled this appointment, I could forget coming home with her for Christmas that year. Shawna and I met in first grade and we kept each other sane and more or less alive until we could high-tail it out of our small-town East Texas hell. When I came out and my parents decided they didn't have a daughter anymore, Shawna's folks—old hippies who live in a geodesic dome out in the piney woods—became my family. I couldn't not go home with her for Christmas, I would die of loneliness. So here I was, scanning the booths for this mysterious Wade. Shawna said I would know him when I saw him.

A young mom with a baby—nope. Two elderly women lingering over coffee—nope. A gentleman wearing a smart western shirt, a black leather and turquoise bolero tie, well-worn, lovingly polished snakeskin boots, his summer cowboy hat on the seat beside him—oh my god. Not a gentleman, I mean, he—she—*was* a gentleman, but she—he—was techni-cally not a man. I mean, well. It's complicated, and I should know. But when I first saw him, I assumed Wade was a man, and I about lost my nerve completely. The only thing that stopped me from bolting was remembering how Shawna's mom always hugged me tight and kissed my forehead and said, "And *here's* our handsome Daisy!" Wade saw me and crooked a finger. I slumped shyly into the seat across from him, leaping to my feet again as he rose to shake my hand. It was only when, smiling, he said, "You must be Daisy," speaking clearly and with authority in his mellow alto drawl that I realized he was a woman.

We talked for over an hour, Wade gently coaxing me to tell him about myself. He spoke admiringly of Shawna and listened kindly to my lame attempts to recount some sort of amusing tale relating to high school (it was rarely amusing in high school, believe me). He told me he worked with FTMs to help them perfect a masculine demeanor, but that he himself identified as Old School Butch, and his most preferred job was consulting for emerging butches. "And I never say 'baby butch,' Daisy," he told me gravely. "You are far from being a baby." I couldn't stop looking at him, at his neatly pressed shirt that lay flat across his chest (how did he *do* that? all my attempts with Ace bandages and sports bras were nothing but failures), his crisp jeans, the chunky men's watch that rested easily on his wrist. Every so often, through the heavy air filled with food smells, I caught a whiff of his cologne, something high-end and manly. I felt intensely embarrassed and unkempt and hopeful all at the same time. Shawna, as usual, had been absolutely correct. I needed Wade. But could I afford him?

It turned out Wade worked on a kind of barter/honor system. I paid what I could now, and later, after I was out of school and launched in life, I promised to keep in touch and to be available if he ever needed my skills. It sounded medieval, like I was his serf or bond slave or something. I immediately agreed to everything and we shook.

"Let me take care of the bill," he said as we prepared to leave, having set a date to meet again the next week. "Watch carefully."

He beckoned the waitress over, flirted pleasantly with her, extracted an elegant leather wallet from his hip pocket and left the exact amount, with a generous tip. Pure poetry.

Wade worked me for months. When I think back on it, I still feel mortified about the sorry picture of a butch he saw when we first met, but he was used to guys who weren't quite together yet, and he never made me feel bad. He had a fatherly way of looking me over, so nonjudgmental, just practical, like, "Hmm, I bet a Yale would make Daisy look even more dashing; it would bring out his features more," instead of, "Lord Jesus, we have to do something about that pitiful scraggly-ass haircut!" Our first lesson was on style. Wade said, "Now some guys do well with the grunge look, but I think you, Daisy, are more a suit-and-tie sort of butch." Who knew? But he was right, of course. He taught me never to leave the house without ironing my jeans, never to wear T-shirts in public unless I was playing softball, and to always make sure my boots were shined. He helped me order a binder that would actually work and gave me tips about undershirts. He went through my wardrobe, tossing most of it, then we hit some thrift stores to find good quality men's shirts, ties, and slacks. We made a trip to the department store for some decent cologne, and, most importantly, I used my credit card to order a tailored suit, and never once did I regret the substantial debt incurred.

Wade helped me with dicks, too, and I started packing 24/7. "A lot of guys make the mistake of packing too big for their build," he murmured, that first heady day my soft pack arrived in the mail. "Now you need to decide if you're going to dress to the right or left." Then he explained what he meant.

"I'm very pleased with you, D," Wade said, after watching me flawlessly escort Shawna out of the restaurant where we'd just had supper. I handed her into a taxi, gave the driver the fare, and sent her on her way. She'd acted like she was doing me a big favor, coming with us to play lady to my gentleman, Wade observing and taking note of my form, but I could tell she was enjoying the hell out of it. As the taxi drove off, Wade gave me a fatherly smile.

"You are just about there, son," he said. "There's just one more thing."

I gulped. I knew what he was talking about, and it was giving me fits.

"Now, have you been practicing like I told you?"

"Yes, sir," I managed, my voice squeaky.

"You have everything you need?"

"I do." In my Dopp kit were condoms, the lube Wade had recommended, my precious hard pack, and a little box of honey powder that had caught my eye in a sex toys catalogue.

"You remember our lessons?"

"Yes, sir!" They were burned in my memory, the things he'd spoken of so calmly as we sat in different restaurants around Dallas, his voice pitched low so we couldn't be overheard. He taught me about erogenous zones, how to gauge likes and dislikes, what to do in all manner of intimate situations, opening my eyes to the infinite variety of femme desire.

He reached over to lightly punch my shoulder. "Well, if you're like most guys, you won't remember a thing when it comes right down to it, but I'm glad you were paying attention." He handed me a slip of perfumed paper.

"You're in luck. My dear friend and colleague Vera has expressed interest in you. Pick her up at this address on Friday. I know you'll make me proud."

La Posada was hidden on a side street, a small oasis of cozy, plush booths, dim lighting, soft jazz, and, Wade told me, some of the best food in Dallas. In fact, he helped me preorder a special menu for our meal—all I had to do was tell the waiter my name and the rest would be taken care of. "Won't Vera want to pick her own stuff?" I'd asked, and Wade had smiled. "No, I think she'll enjoy knowing that you've had the foresight to plan a lovely evening for her." He was right. From the grapefruit margarita to the ceviche to the house special involving delicious things I'd never even heard of before, Vera seemed to be thrilled. With each new delicacy, her eyes would widen, her full lips part in anticipation, and she would lean forward to watch the waiter place the dish on the table, murmuring, *"Que rico!"* Watching her was pure delight. I'm not sure I'd ever paid much attention to the way women eat, but Vera was so sensuous, so unabashed in taking her pleasure. I loved how she clapped her hands and bounced a little bit in her chair; I loved being the one who was giving her such enjoyment.

I'd been incredibly nervous when I rang her bell earlier that evening, but right away she managed to distract me, taking both of my hands and kissing my cheek, saying all in a rush how glad she was to meet me, she'd heard such nice things about me from Wade, how *guapo*, how handsome I looked, how hungry she was, a *dónde vamos*, where would we be going? A whole stream of excited words and gestures as she took my arm and followed me to the car. She was at least 5'8", but somehow made me feel like I was the taller one, and I barely had time to be intimidated, even though she was gorgeous and sophisticated, her dark hair falling in shining waves to the middle of her back, her curvy body straining deliciously against the velvety material of her form-fitting dress. By the time we'd gotten to the restaurant, I had stopped checking every five seconds to see if I had my wallet, and was starting to connect to what Wade called "Butch Mind": paying complete attention to this marvelous woman who was talking a mile a minute beside me, but also thinking two and three steps ahead to the logistics of parking, how I would help her out of the car, open the door for her at the restaurant, pull out her chair.

Now the waiter placed dessert on our table with a flourish, a shallow dish containing luscious mounds of tropical fruit sherbet dusted with chocolate and garnished with a fan of paper-thin lemon cookies.

"Exquisito!" Vera breathed. I smiled at her, willing myself not to let my gaze stray from her face. I'd spent the entire date

striving valiantly not to ogle her cleavage—Wade had been very clear on this point—but I couldn't help take a quick peek now and then, and once, I know she caught me; I noticed a tiny, indulgent smile flit across her face, and I blushed. I spent a lot of time blushing, but she was so kindhearted, so attentive and interested in my attempts to make adult conversation, that I managed to forget to be uncomfortable most of the time. And really, I felt good sitting there with her. Settled in my skin. So this was what it was like to be with a femme, to adore her with your eyes and know she likes it, to make things nice for her with careful attention to details. Pamper her.

"*Ay, mira,*" Vera exclaimed, and I snapped back to attention. "They forgot a spoon!"

Sure enough, there was only one of the heavy, long-handled dessert spoons. I was about to call the waiter over when I caught her eye and had a better idea. I picked up the spoon, shaved off a sliver of passion fruit sherbet, and offered it to her. How can I explain this? She welcomed the spoon into her mouth. She held my gaze. Through the smooth handle, I could feel her lips close over the bowl, feel the slight vibration as her tongue curled around the sherbet. With a sigh, she swallowed, then opened her mouth and released the spoon. My hand was trembling, but I fed her until the sherbet was gone.

Back at her apartment, sitting on her big, overstuffed couch, the tremble had reached my whole body. I tried to unclench my teeth, the taste of the dessert wine she'd served me sweet in my mouth. She was beside me, completely at ease, sipping her wine.

"Oh, that was such a delicious meal!" she said. "*Mil gracias, lindo.*"

"It was my pleasure." My voice was shaking. I was thinking I had better go home. Stop while I was ahead and not waste any more of her time. Even though Wade had said they worked together, that she had a very special and important role that she enjoyed and did willingly, I didn't feel like going through with it anymore. I was feeling like a loser all over again, just a fool East Texas redneck, a backwoods hick. I tensed, thinking I would stand up and go, and that's when Vera reached over and loosened my tie. *"Mmm, papito,"* she whispered. She tugged gently on my tie and I leaned over her, engulfed in her warmth, the scent of her woodsy perfume, the nameless something she exuded and that I needed more than anything I'd ever needed in my life.

When her lips touched mine, her whole body seemed to surge toward me, although she didn't move except to settle herself more comfortably against the cushions. It wasn't a desperate kiss, although I was feeling desperate, but there was a quiet power about it, a promise. Her arms went around me, her fingers danced through my hair. She teased the tender skin of my scalp with her long nails, and my entire body broke out in goose bumps. I got an instant erection—I mean, I could *feel* my soft pack lengthen and harden, and what's more, I swear she could, too, because she wiggled and sighed, and her breathing quickened. The whole thing freaked me out so much—the way that inanimate object had suddenly become fully a part of my body—that I pulled away. I didn't even think how that might offend or upset her, but she just smiled dreamily at me, stretching her legs out in front of her, letting her high heels dangle from her toes. *"Corazón,"* she continued, putting one hand on my trembling thigh. "My feet *me duelen*, after all day in these shoes..." In a second, I was on my knees before her, gently removing her pumps. Wade taught me that a gentleman is always ready to offer relief to a lady in the form of massage, so I had practiced ad nauseam on Shawna. As I rubbed and caressed Vera's feet, she melted even further into the couch. I was doing that. I was making her feel like that.

I was placing a soft kiss on the bottom of her instep when Vera softly stroked my head, then reached down and took my hand. I rose, helping her from the couch. She came into my arms as we stood there, allowing me to pull her close so I could feel her breasts, her soft belly, her thighs and mound. Before I could panic again, she made one of her little satisfied sounds, a variation of which she'd been making on and off all evening, at the ceviche, at the wine, at the dessert she had eaten from my spoon.

"You smell so good," she said into my neck. "You feel so good." She leaned against me, soft and willing, and I knew that she was waiting for me, that whatever I did, however I proceeded, she would follow my lead. "Flying on a wing and a prayer," that's what my Gramps used to say about impossible situations, and that's what I decided to do now. I held her close to me, then gently let her go, keeping hold of her hand. I led her into the bedroom, where there were candles and air-conditioning and a pissed-off cat who left angrily with her tail in the air. I sat Vera on the bed, I said, "Wait here, beautiful. Don't move," and quickly went out to the car, got my bag, stopped off in the bathroom, and made my way back to her. She hadn't moved.

"What a good girl," I found myself saying—was that me, that firm voice? "What a good, sweet girl you are."

She smiled up at me and then we were together on the bed and I was cupping her ass cheeks, pulling her up against my dick, my hands everywhere, on her legs, her back, her beautiful breasts, her shoulders. My fingers smoothing her hair, going in and out of her mouth as she moved under me, pushing up, moaning and sighing, pulling my suit jacket off my shoulders as I slid her dress up, exposing her thighs and lacy panties. The talkative, excited girl was gone, replaced by a luminous woman, lush and pliant beneath me. I wrenched the dress off over her head, but left on her underthings. She shivered slightly, so I kissed her mouth and then kissed her all over, holding her head with my hands, reassuring her. When I kissed her thighs I could smell her excitement, see the damp soaking through the pink lace, and I kissed her there. She moved under my mouth, my dick jumped in my pants, and suddenly we were both working to undo my belt, my breath coming hard and her voice a low moan. I reached for the condom I'd transferred to my pants pocket earlier and managed to slide it on, her fingers patting and smoothing alongside mine. In my delirium, that dainty strip of sodden lace over her pussy became a huge barrier—how was I supposed to get past that? I didn't think I could wait long enough to pull her panties down, I wanted to get inside her so bad, and then she was stroking me with one hand, pulling the lace aside with the other, her knees falling apart, and I was close, so close, my dick throbbing and pulsing, she was arching up to me, opening for me, guiding my dick head so that, almost before I knew what was happening, I was there, all the way up to my balls, engulfed, encompassed, surrounded, out of my mind. My fists in her hair, kissing her, inhaling her, I fucked her with such abandon, grunting, rutting, calling her name, crying out when her fingernails went up under my shirt and raked the skin between my shoulder blades, dazed electrified, on fire. She in turn, found her voice, encouraging me with a nonstop sexy monologue: *Ven, mi hombre, te quiero así, aquí, encima de mí, con tu fuerza, tu cuerpo de hombre, así me gusta, mi cuerpo está para tí, más más ahí...*

She wrapped around me, her legs pulling me close, heels drumming on my ass, her arms spread wide at times, hands gripping the sides of the bed, at other times roaming over my back, scratching me, slapping at me in ecstasy. I abandoned myself in her, to her, and the more she gave in to me, the more I found I was able to give to her, as she rode my dick to a frantic, scream of a come and then a more gentle one. I could feel the pull of her orgasms on my dick and then I was coming, too, shooting deep inside her, feeling it start as a tightening in my balls and then a great whooshing release, my whole body jerking and vibrating on top of her as she opened and opened for me.

And then I was in her arms as she kissed away my tears. She cuddled against me, let me hold her and cry, and then, when I had calmed down, she went into the bathroom and came back looking wicked and wanton with her underthings all askew, wearing what she said was her cocksucking lipstick, and it started up again and it went on all night. We used the honey powder and all of the items she had in her bedside drawer and we didn't fall asleep until the sky outside her window was beginning to lighten.

Every single thing we did that night is precious to me. But there's one moment that stands out, and I think about it a lot, even now that I've graduated from Wade's butch tutorial and can do Butch Mind as a matter of course, and what's more, I have occasion to use my training, as I've gotten to where I can find regular dates. The thing I hold closest these days, now that Wade and I are bros and colleagues and I have my own place in the brotherhood of butch gentlemen around Dallas; what I remember most, now that Vera has moved on, gotten married up in Massachusetts to a fast-talking Yankee butch, one lucky bastard who came down here on a job and left with one of our finest flowers; the thing I think about and hold dear in my heart when I'm alone and in a meditative mood, is this: Vera, standing in her doorway in her red kimono robe, saying good-bye to me. Her hair is a crazy mess, she looks gorgeous and well fucked. Her lips, their own lovely pink color as the lipstick has long since been rubbed off, are swollen from their long session wrapped around my dick.

Taking my face in both her hands, she kisses me one last time, soft, and then softer, such a joyous kiss that it is this one sweet moment that I treasure most from that most memorable of evenings because it said, more than anything else: Hello. Here you are. *Bienvenido*.

THIS IS WHAT I WANT

CS Clark

One

This is what I want. This is not what I want. This, you, every-thing you give to me. Everything you take without asking.

I know I asked for this.

I know we talked about it beforehand, all that consensual shit we said in the light of day, in the comfort of your arms, in our bed. But I do not want this now. Now that it's real, now that it's really going to happen. And I cannot bring myself to ask you to stop now that we've begun.

I am wearing my short skirt and knee-highs. My shirt, my socks, my panties, everything crisp and new and white. We are sitting on the couch, casually watching a movie, a bowl of chips in your lap. Well, that's not right, exactly: You are sitting casually. I am pretending, feeling taut as stretched wire. We are watching a cartoon movie, all pinafores and smiling cats and off with their heads. I'm looking at the screen, but what I'm really watching is you, trying to read you, trying to gauge what comes next and when. Every now and then you look at me, smiling, put your hand on my knee and ask me if I like the movie, if I'm having fun. I nod and smile. I can't believe how shy I feel, how not like myself at all.

You ask me to slide closer, tell me Daddy is getting a little lonely in the corner all by himself. As I move across the couch, my skirt creeps up a little. You let your hand linger there, in the spot you were patting on the couch to indicate where you wanted me, your warm hand and your thumb barely moving against the side of my thigh. Your eyes stay there, too, just a beat long enough to make me uncomfortable, a blush spreading from my cheeks to the roots of my hair. Then you meet my gaze again, the smile turning into that easy laugh of yours, the one that puts people at ease, that says there's not a care in the world worth mentioning. The laugh I secretly get jealous over whenever I hear you share it with others. You gently stroke my hair and put your arm around me, pull me closer to you, the bowl of snacks gone. It is suddenly very warm in this room.

Your attention is turned back toward the movie, but I can feel a change in your breathing, sitting so close to you like this. You play with the ends of my hair, something any Daddy might do, doting on his little girl. I feel myself relaxing a bit, hoping that perhaps this is as far as we will go tonight, that at any moment we will drop the game and turn back into ourselves. Praying that we won't.

I feel you turn your face toward my neck, inhaling the scent of my hair, your hot breath just under my ear. *Such a pretty little girl*, you say, *so clean. So pretty.* And I know we are not going to stop this, and god help me, I can feel myself go wetter and wetter with each exhale. *Give Daddy a kiss, baby girl.* I turn to you, the chastest of kisses on my lips. You brush mine delicately, touch my mouth with the tip of your tongue. I jerk back. You chuckle again, this time much lower in your throat, your hand never leaving the back of my neck, kissing me deeper. I can smell your cologne, bay rum, mingled with the whiskey you drank earlier, a trace of cigarette smoke. Your breath in my ear: *Touch it like Daddy showed you.* Oh god. Oh god oh god oh god. Your hand on mine, moving it toward your lap, your other hand unzipping your fly.

The whimper that escapes from me is a surprise to myself. I turn my face away, try to withdraw my hand. *Come on, love. Be a good girl.*

I will, Daddy. I will, I promise, just please don't make me. Please don't make me touch it.

I can beg all I want, but your hand is already around mine, directing my fingers to your cock, stroking the shaft up and down slowly, a low moan voicing your approval. *That's it, baby girl. That's so nice, just the way your Daddy likes it.* Now it's my breathing that changes, quickening in my chest. You're still holding my hand loosely in your own, but even if you weren't I wouldn't stop. I'm not hoping we'll stop. Not anymore. I let my hand move gently, only stroking faster when you prompt me to, remembering my ruse of innocence. I am watching your face, your eyes closed and head leaned back, and all I want to do is please my Daddy. I barely notice you reaching for the lube. Your hand opens mine and you pour a little over the head, grabbing my hand and directing me. I keep the pace you've set, stroking your hard cock, the veined silicone jerking a little under my touch. Knowing you won't be able to take much more of this without coming, wanting to make you. Now I am trying to hold myself back a little. I know how to jack my Daddy off proper, but your sweet little girl is not supposed to. You're watching me looking at you, at my hand on your dick, watching the motion, my effect on you. Gone from shy girl to fascination in a matter of minutes. I want to see it, want to see you come all over my fist, see you lose control and know I made it happen, made you feel that good.

But you stop me. Put your hand on mine and stop me, saying that's enough for now, and I am a little disappointed, a little excited about what might happen next, not quite sure what you want from me.

C'mere, baby. Come and sit on Daddy's lap. I sidle over to you, try to straddle and face you but you turn me around, my back to your chest. You say nothing. Your hands are everywhere, slow and delicate, but everywhere, all over me. Sliding over my knees, up my thighs. Unbuttoning two, now three buttons on my shirt, running over my nipples in my cotton training bra that's too small for me, my tits spilling out into your hands, nipples hard as pebbles at your touch. Over my belly, down my hips. You groan, rub your hard-on against my ass in your lap. Your hands on my thighs, reaching just to the edge of my panties, tracing their outline over and over again until I want to... I don't even know what I want. The torture is too delicious. I want you to do that forever, drown us both in me. Want you to touch me, fuck me, anything. Anything. My hips pushing against you more insistently, trying to get contact between your hand and my pussy, my ass grinding into you now, both of us panting.

Daddy. It hurts.

What hurts, baby?

It hurts. Down there.

Here? Your fingers rubbing my hard little clit through my panties. Tracing the outlines of my pussy as I press into you.

My, my. Seems we have a very bad, very wet little girl here, now don't we? Is this where it hurts? Is this where you want me to make it better?

Uh-huh. Oh god, Daddy. Please.

Please.

You slide my panties to the side, your fingers all over me. I am soaking wet, know I will be in trouble later for ruining the brand-new pair of panties you bought me, which makes me even wetter. I am moaning, calling out *Papi, Daddy*, calling your name.

At the sound of it your hand stops and you heave a sigh. *I'm sorry, Daddy*, I manage to quickly stutter, but too late. I know your real name is not allowed here. Your hand comes down none too gently on me, slapping the clit you were just stroking; the repeated, stinging slaps exciting me even more, your flat hand smacking then touching then hitting again. The blows lighten and alternate with fondling, clit to pussy and back again, circling around the edges of me. Your other hand yanks the fabric aside, your touch everywhere. My clit is on fire as you circle it with one hand, finger me with the other.

Daddy. Daddy, please. It hurts so much now. Please.

Please what?

Please make it stop.

You want me to stop?

No! I...

You ache. You burn. You feel like you're on fire, like you're going to explode...

Your finger circling my clit faster now as you whisper in my ear, raising me to a fever pitch. I can't take it. It feels so good I almost can't stand it.

Daddy's got something for you, baby. Something very special for you.

You lift me enough to push my skirt up in the back, your hand underneath me now, your pants down, your cock even harder than before, fingers still rubbing at me, my panties shoved out of your way, possibly torn. A few more movements and you are inside me, making me gasp at how quickly you fill me. You rock me on your lap, grab me by my ass, move me up and down, your hips rising to meet each stroke. I struggle, not because I want to get away, but because I know you'll slam me harder if I do, pull me down onto you until you're so deep I can feel you in my belly. I try to pull away. You grab my waist, my hips, pummel me. Suddenly I am pitched forward, bent over the coffee table, you fucking me from behind, pinning me there with your weight, my wrists in your hands at my sides. Fuck me, Daddy. Fuck me.

You rise up, spreading my ass cheeks as you fuck me with long, deep strokes to the core of me. You move my right hand to my clit, tell me to touch myself while you fuck me. I am molten, electric. The base of your dick and balls slapping my ass as you tell me, *Come. Come now, you little slut. Come all over Daddy's big dick in your cunt.* And I do, orgasm building from the center of my spine and out, out to the tips of my fingers, down my legs and into my ass, screaming from beginning to end. You don't alter your pace in the slightest, just fuck me harder and harder until I think I might break, rug burns on my knees and your final thrust pushing me so hard into the coffee table I'll have bruises on my hips for days as you fill me, calling out, *Good girl. That's Daddy's sweet little girl, Daddy's little slut. Take it, baby, take it for Daddy.*

And I do.

Two

These are things I know about you: the shape of the indentation above your lip. The way your arm feels, thrown over me while we sleep. How you smell after an hour-long workout. The way the bulge in your jeans makes you swagger, and the looks you sometimes get near public bathrooms. Your minor obsession with the English teacher that drove you crazy all through the tenth grade. That you are due home in twenty minutes or so, and I am ready.

I finish buttoning up, taking a last look in the mirror. Sheer blouse, just see-through enough to show a bit of the lace bra I'm wearing underneath. Long pencil skirt, pin-striped with a deep slit up one side. Back-seam stockings, garter belt, pearls, glasses I don't really wear. Very un-sensible shoes. Teachers never looked like this where I went to school, but then again, this isn't your average lesson plan, though I certainly have plans of instilling a bit of knowledge in you tonight. I wonder if you'll be naughty or good. Both contingencies are planned for.

I hear your key in the door, the familiar noises you make on arrival. Your voice calling out for me. Without answering I step out and into the living room, making exactly the entrance I want as you fumble with your things, almost dropping most of them as you cast a long look my way.

Please find appropriate attire laid out for you in the other room. Change, and, young man? Wipe that insipid grin off your face.

Yes, Ma'am.

You manage the correct response, dropping your eyes, unable to stop smiling. As you brush past me, I catch you sneaking a glance at my legs. Bad boi.

In the kitchen, I pour myself a glass of wine, thankful that I'm the one able to drink in this role, giving you time to change, time to think about what I'm up to.

I give the door to the bedroom a quiet knock, pushing it open without asking if you're decent first. A pleasant surprise, you waiting patiently at your desk, already dressed. Even your posture is to be commended. Score a couple of points for you.

I remember finding that desk at one of those huge summer flea markets, both of us thinking how my nieces would love to have one to play school with. We bought two, then at the last minute gave them the first and kept the second for ourselves. Now I'm extra glad we did.

Seeing you like this—polo shirt, dark pants, hair pushed back from your face, and your eyes gleaming—you look almost as young as you are pretending to be. I could climb on top of that desk, straddle and fuck you right now, or slide underneath it, unzip your pants, and suck your dick, which I'm quite sure is hard for me already. But I won't. It's more fun to make you earn it, make you wait. So instead I stroll around your desk, making sure the angles give you a good view of my legs and ass as I move past you and take a seat. I busy myself at my own makeshift desk, rearranging some papers, moving some things around. Nothing important, just stalling, knowing that while I'm virtually ignoring you, you are incapable of doing anything but gazing at me expectantly. I do so enjoy having you in my thrall.

Well, Mr. St. James, it seems you've found your way to your seat. Are we ready to begin our lesson?

Yes, Ms. Moreno. I mean—yes, ma'am. I'm ready to begin.

Very good, then. I believe today's lesson will start with some review of the poets we've been working with. Please read aloud.

Your voice falters only slightly.

"This is the line between us
Faded now into shadow, smudged soft as coal dust.
We merge and fall back to ourselves
Slowly
This tender ache in me,
Your name and your absence."

I can hear the desire in your voice, the slight rasp hinting at your lust and expectation. I am standing near you now, trailing my fingertips across the desktop, coming to rest on your paper, leaning over and into you. We are not touching, but I am close enough for you to feel the heat radiating off me and to get a good look down my shirt.

That was...lovely. Tell me what you think the author of this poem is trying to convey. Give me your particular insight into the meaning of this poem for you.

My breath warm near your neck as I speak. I pull back far enough to make eye contact, hold your gaze as I wait for your answer.

Well, Ms., um, Ms. Moreno. What I think is that, uh, that what the author is trying to say, what he or she is getting at, is the thread of pain in desire. When two people, uh, merge passionately, there is a sort of communion. And when that moment is over it's almost painful to return to reality, to return to the loneliness of being just one. But that pain is what fuels the desire for connection, over and over.

Why, Mr. St. James—are you suggesting that this poem is about fucking?

Well, I...I certainly think it's referencing making love, if that's what you mean.

So you're saying I had you read a poem about fucking? Call a spade a spade, dear student. Are you saying your teacher would give you such...suggestive material?

My hand is on my blouse now, running slowly over my shoulders, down my breasts, hovering lightly over my nipples. You stutter and backpedal, more talk of "making love" and "sexual union," some nonsense of the sort. Me, I'm just watching your face get redder and redder as I unbutton the first two buttons of my blouse, nodding as I listen to you struggle for words.

Stand up, St James. Come here.

I, um. I...can't right now, Ms. Moreno.

I walk back to you, lean down into your ear, pressing my tits up against your arm.

I've been watching you, young man. Watching you look at me. Don't think I haven't noticed the way you stare at my tits, my legs. I can even feel your eyes on my ass when I walk away.

I reach under the desk, finding your bulging hard package waiting for me as you take in air, an unexpected gasp.

Tsk tsk tsk. Naughty boi. Is this any way to show respect for your teacher, by getting such a raging hard-on? Well, lucky for you, I know what bois like you want, what you need. Come here.

I stand and pull you up with me, put your hand on my shirt and instruct you to undo the remaining buttons, and I swear to god you're trembling. I'm so wet I can feel it on the inside of my thighs. I clench them together, trying to stay focused. Your eyes glued to my tits, I ask if you'd like to touch them, place first one hand then the other on my chest, letting you fondle and grope for a few minutes, finally pulling my lacy bra down under them and shoving your face in my cleavage. Your mouth is wild on me, tasting and devouring every inch of my breasts, pulling my nipples gently then harder, sucking in all the skin around them. Teeth and tongue and mouth and oh god I think I could come just like this, just keep doing this. We're both gasping and panting, your mouth seemingly on my tits, my neck, my mouth all at once, but I stop you, push you away.

I pull out my desk chair, sit down, reach for your belt, and pull it off in one smooth motion. Your pants are down and off next and I can tell you think you're about to get blown, but oh, no. I pat my lap.

C'mere, boi. It seems you need a little discipline, a little lesson in respect.

As you lie across my legs, I pull your underwear down but not off. My god, but you are a beautiful young man, your ass wiggling around in my lap as you struggle for contact with my thigh. The slit on my skirt is pushed up and open, and I wonder how long it would take you to come with your dick rubbing against my stocking, my leg. I start with my hand, caressing, and then the first smack comes out of nowhere. You buck a little, letting me know you felt it and, as you do, catching another smack on the way down.

Such bad, bad manners. Such a dirty mind. Another smack, then another. My hand goes behind me, reaching for the ruler I've tucked out of sight. *You should be ashamed of yourself, thinking such nasty things about your teacher.* I hit you three times in quick succession with the ruler, reaching with my other hand to stroke your cock as I spank you, over and over. *I bet this is what you do when you think about me, isn't it? Lying in bed at night, all alone in your room, your hand on your dick. Do you jack off and think about me? You do, don't you? Say it.*

You moan and rock, saying yes, yes, trying to tell me all the dirty things you fantasize about doing to me when you touch yourself, but mostly it just comes out in pants, a few nasty words sprinkled in here and there. I'm building a steady rhythm now, one hand wrapped around your dick and the other raining blows down on you as you thrust into my fist and I am soaking fucking wet and that's it, I can't take it anymore. I push you off me and down to the floor, unzipping my skirt, tossing it aside and straddling you, grateful I didn't wear panties, shoving your cock all the way in. Your hands run furiously up and down my legs. I pull one leg forward and around to the top of you, my foot next to your head as you turn, kissing and licking my shoe, sucking my toes through the nylon. I slide the heel into your mouth, in and out as I ride you, leaning back on my hands and moaning out what a good boi you are, what a good, nasty, delicious fucking boi as I come all over you, you calling out *Ms. Moreno, Ms. Moreno* the whole time.

And this, this is exactly what I want. Both of us like this and every other way we can think of being. Do it again.

ABOUT THE AUTHORS

VALERIE ALEXANDER is a writer who lives in Arizona. Her work has been previously published in *Best Lesbian Erotica*, *Best of Best Women's Erotica*, and other anthologies.

CRYSTAL BARELA (writingisseduction@blogspot.com) is a writer, dreamer, reader who creates art, laughter, flirtation. She likes glitter, graffiti, rainbows, and girls in fishnets who can swing a hammer. Nature, music, dancing, and well-crafted erotica are her faves.

KATHLEEN BRADEAN would like to whisper depraved suggestions into your ear while stealing your wallet. Her stories can be found in *Carnal Machines: Steampunk Erotica*, *Best Women's Erotica*, *Best Lesbian Fiction 2008*, *The Sweetest Kiss*, and many other anthologies. Find her on EroticaRevealed. com, OhGetAGrip.com, and KathleenBradean.Blogspot.com.

RACHEL KRAMER BUSSEL (rachelkramerbussel.com) is a New York–based author, editor, and blogger. She is senior editor at *Penthouse Variations* and hosts the In The Flesh reading series. Her books include *Best Bondage Erotica 2012, Orgasmic, Fast Girls, Passion, The Mile High Club, Bottoms Up, Spanked, Peep Show, Tasting Him,* and more.

CS CLARK is a musician, artist, and author living in Chicago. She has been published previously in *Best Lesbian Erotica 2008*.

ANDREA DALE's (cyvarwydd.com) work appeared in the Lambda Award–winning anthology *Lesbian Cowboys: Erotic Adventures* and the *Romantic Times* 4.5-star anthology *Fairy Tale Lust*, as well as about 100 other anthologies. She'd wear comfy clothes to win a contest but dresses up sexy for rock concerts.

CHARLOTTE DARE's (www.myspace.com/charlotte_dare) fiction publications include *Best Lesbian Erotica 2011, Best Lesbian Romance 2011, Lesbian Cowboys,* and *Where the Girls Are: Urban Lesbian Erotica.* She dedicates this story to Anna, the love of her life.

SHANNA GERMAIN (www.shannagermain.com) believes that the best dogs, like the best partners, arrive when we're not looking. Her stories have appeared in places like *Best American Erotica, Best Gay Bondage, Best Gay Erotica, Best Gay Romance, Best Lesbian Erotica, Best Lesbian Romance,* and more.

Performance poet **AIMEE HERMAN** edits for Oysters & Chocolate and has performed at In the Flesh erotic salon, Queer Lit Carnival, and The Red Umbrella Diaries in NYC. Find her in *Best Lesbian Love Stories* (Alyson Books), *Best Women's Erotica 2010* (Cleis), and *Nice Girls, Naughty Sex* (Seal).

RIVER LIGHT is a writer and sex educator from Vancouver, Canada. When not tending to her family she writes and reads porn, teaches kink workshops, and creates scenes. Her erotica can be found in a variety of anthologies. She is working on a book of essays and stories.

ELAINE MILLER (ElaineMiller.com) is a Vancouver leath-erdyke who has been passionately involved in the leather/queer/sexuality community for eighteen years through writing, education, and creating gathering space. A writer of fiction and nonfiction, Elaine has been frequently anthologized and spent four years as the regular kinky sex columnist for Xtra West.

EVAN MORA is a femme writer living in Toronto, and wants to state that although the bar and Butch/Femme salon are both real, and although she did in fact attend the Speakeasy edition of the salon...this story is entirely fictitious. No really, it is. Find her in lots of anthologies.

TERESA NOELLE ROBERTS creates erotica for horny roman-tics of all persuasions. Her short fiction has appeared in *Best Bondage Erotica 2011*, *Orgasmic*, *Best of the Best Women's Erotica 2*, *The Sweetest Kiss*, *Lesbian Lust*, and many anthol-ogies with similar eyebrow-raising titles. She writes erotic romance for Samhain and Phaze.

MIEL ROSE is a queer, rural, working-class high femme. Besides a smut writer, she is a fashion designer and an assistant stylist. Her butch/femme love and sex stories can be found in

Best Lesbian Erotica 2008, Lesbian Lust, and the upcoming *Best Lesbian Romance 2011,* to name a few.

STELLA SANDBERG is a Swedish writer of queer erotica, preferably in the genre of historical pulp pastiche. She is published in the anthologies *Best Lesbian Erotica 2010, Where the Girls Are, Working Girls,* and *Island Girls.*

SINCLAIR SEXSMITH (mrsexsmith.com) writes *Sugarbutch Chronicles: The Sex, Gender, and Relationship Adventures of a Kinky Queer Butch Top* at sugarbutch.net and has been published in various anthologies and on numerous websites, including the *Best Lesbian Erotica* series and *Persistence: All Ways Butch and Femme.* She lives in New York City.

ANNA WATSON is an Old School femme married to her Old School butch, raising two marvelous boys. For more about butches and femmes, sex and being human, see *Take Me There, Sometimes She Lets Me, Femmethology, vol. 1,* and *Girl Crazy.* Thanks to Samantha in Chile for the sexy Spanish!

Multipublished erotica author **BETH WYLDE** (www.beth-wylde.com) writes what she likes to read, which includes a little bit of everything. Her muse is an equal-opportunity plot bunny that believes everyone, no matter their kink, color, gender, or orientation, is entitled to love, acceptance, and scalding HOT sex.

ABOUT
THE EDITOR

D. L. KING spends an inordinate amount of time reading and writing smut in her New York City apartment and postage-stamp-sized-garden. *The Harder She Comes: Butch/Femme Erotica* is her fourth anthology with Cleis Press. She is the editor of *Carnal Machines: Steampunk Erotica, The Sweetest Kiss: Ravishing Vampire Erotica* and the Lambda Literary Award Finalist, *Where the Girls Are: Urban Lesbian Erotica.* She is also the editor of *Spank!,* a Logical Lust anthology. D. L. King is the publisher and editor of the erotica review site, Erotica Revealed, which has been referred to as the "*New York Times* Book Review of Erotica." The author of dozens of short stories, her work can be found in various editions of *Best Lesbian Erotica, Best Women's Erotica, The Mammoth Book of Best New Erotica,* as well as such titles as *Fast Girls, Girl Crazy, Broadly Bound, Gotta Have It, Sex in the City: New York, Please Ma'am, Sweet Love,* and *Frenzy,* among others. She is the author of two novels of female domination and male submission, *The Melinoe Project* and *The Art of Melinoe*. Find out more at dlkingerotica.blogspot.com and dlkingerotica.com.

Printed in the United States
by Baker & Taylor Publisher Services